Jack Crow Knows

A relatable tale by Kathy LaFollett

Thank you for your
thoughts, ideas, and
fresh perspective ♡

ISBN – 9781709408694

For my children, that they should always live in wonder.

For my husband, who told me, "Just write!"

For my parents, that allowed me the longitude and latitude.

For my sisters who are, and ever shall be, banned from my room.

"They aren't that smart." A fair judgement after three weeks of observation and attempted communication. Jack perched on his viewing chair, looking through the glass window, continuing his wait while taking mental notes.

"How could they be dangerous if they are this slow? They seem eager enough to learn." Jack hopped to a different chair to watch for her reaction to the four shells he placed in her view …all these chairs and tables out here on this porch, yet no one was eating on any of it. Jack shifted positions, in case she wasn't paying attention. Sometimes it was hard to tell if they were paying attention.

Jack noted her ability to jump when called. That would come in handy. But she wasn't grasping the whole seashell-offerings-for-food idea. He'd gotten a cat to trade a bowl of delicious cat food for a stick once. He had to find a dead mouse to impale on the stick, but the cat made the trade. Jack considered the efforts he put into trading things. Some were easier than others. While others were futile attempts at lunch.

The woman behind the window spoke through the glass to him. The windowpane muffled her words. She looked at his shells and nodded.

Humans put faith in the wink and nod. They seem to use it no matter who they were trying to communicate with, or what they were communicating. A wink or nod guaranteed nothing. Humans were downright unreliable.

"I hope she doesn't bring that chunky stuff again." Jack shifted in his thoughts jumping another chair waiting for her to come out with something better than that chunky chalky stuff.

She was having a hard time grasping the four-seashells-equals-peanut-butter-on-those-cracker-chunks order. There were no shells for pellet chunk orders. He knew her problem. He counted at least four flying colored birds in that house. They threw those chalky chunky pellets on the floor as often as he dreaded seeing them on one of these tables. Jack wondered why she kept bringing them to both her birds and him. Nobody liked them. He hopped to another chair.

This human training idea would take time. He'd already invested three weeks into this one. He had to get her straightened out before finding a partner and making a nest. Jack was counting on having a trained human to impress the ladies. Or was he trying to impress his father and buy time? Hard to say, but in either event, right now training was moving slow. Humans just aren't that smart.

He hopped to another chair waiting for his order. When does slow service fall into the bad service category? His buddy Jerry took a girl on a date to a farmhouse last fall. Something convinced him the service was fast and delicious. Big mistake. The old human brought plates of leftover lunch. The old man liked his deviled hams with chopped onion and toasted breads. Jerry didn't see her again after that lunch fiasco. She avoided him at the murder foraging lunches and roost naps. Jerry referred to that day as 'The Close Call' when discussing the farmhouse incident.

"I should bring Todd with me once I have this human trained. To make sure I'm right about the service." The thought finished itself when she came out onto the deck.

"Hi Jack! I made peanut butter on flax crackers for you. Thank you for my seashells." She smiled and laid out square crackers in a row, each smeared with peanut butter.

She then picked up the shells, one by one, and dropped them back into the bonsai pot Jack had pulled them out of. She smiled to Jack and walked through the windowed door to go back into her house.

Jack jumped over to inspect the serving sizes and count. If you can't split dinner up evenly things get awkward on a date. Dates double all the thinking required to do anything. If it's just yourself, well then, that's one brain coming up with ideas. You ask a girl out then the thoughts double as well as the potential for problems. Keeping food and keels even was mandatory for dating. The count was an odd three, but the food was what he ordered. Snack service was half way right and he could fix the former with more training visits. He ate mindfully aware his human training was far from over.

Human training has been in place since the first human interacted with a wild being. The humans tell stories of wolves learning how to be more human. As if that was possible. While the wild things tell the story of Dave and his human. Dave was not a wolf. Wolves found humans inappropriate on every level; useless, slow, inconvenient.

Dave was a weasel. He met his human in his weasel cave having witnessed the man stumbling into his cave carrying a dead thing. It is said that Dave witnessed his human eat the thing, wipe his face on a rock, and fall asleep next to the carcass. To any other wild thing this would set off a chain reaction of screaming and running out of the cave. To Dave's way of thinking this was his cave and this human snoring at his doorway offered an opportunity. If he could harness it's power, focus it on tasks Dave needed doing and trade these outcomes for behaviors that were tolerable, well that would be quite the lifestyle upgrade.

Dave waited for the human to wake up to harness all it's potential. The story told down the ages of wild things says Dave built a mound of sticks and wood and dried grass. He created this close to the snoring human. He then went down to the rolling creek just a quarter mile south and found two flint rocks. He laid them in the sun to dry and ate lunch from the hidden quail nest at the water's edge. Once the flint rocks were dry, he went back to his cave with the dried flint rocks, pulled up a flat stone and sat on it. He watched the sleeping human waiting for him to wake.

Not long before sunset the human roused sitting up to look out the cave. Dave barked. (This is probably where the humans got the idea that a wolf was involved. Weasels bark, humans refuse to accept this fact.) The human looked down at the wild thing looking up. Dave threw the flint rocks at his pile of sticks, woods, and grass with great weasel force. They knocked hard against each other throwing sparks, which caught the grass, which caught the sticks, which caught the wood. Dave crossed his arms and nodded toward the fire erupting flames of orange and red. The human stared at Dave, then the fire. Dave stared at the human and made a thumbing gesture to the fire. The human stared at Dave.

They weren't that smart, these humans. Dave spent the better part of a two seasons getting his human in shape, so the history goes. Overtime Dave the Weasel's story set the benchmark to human training. Two seasons investment was fair. If the human couldn't catch onto things, best to move on. No need spinning one's wheels as they say.

Jack held to this principle of human training. Three weeks was not two seasons. He had time. And he was ready for a nap.

*****

"Where you been?" Todd looked up long enough to see Jack land on his branch and returned to eating his turtle egg.

"Are you going to swallow that thing? It smells like death!"

"It smells like death because it is dead."

Jack, having known Todd since fledgling, also knew this was a rhetorical question. Todd will eat that egg because he knew it was part dead turtle. Todd knew it because he found it on the ground, grabbed it in his mouth, dripping and all, and flew back to his favorite branch to eat it. So yes, talking to his best friend was an exercise in monologue. It was also an exercise in not throwing up.

"So where you been? Want some?" Todd grinned and swallowed. Dripping dead turtle fell from his beak. That last question was rhetorical.

"No, thank you. I just had a splendid clean not dead meal at the yellow house with the lady human. A meal of peanut butter on crackers thank you very much. It only cost four sea shells I didn't have to find. There was a pile of them right there." His meal made more sense than Todd's dead drippy turtle.

"Yeah?" Todd swallowed a final beak full and released the unfinished portion of his dead turtle egg meal. They watched it slide off the branch and fall 40 feet to the ground at the base of the pine tree. "Well, I'm impressed with your fancy served eats there, Jack. I didn't have to line up anything for mine." Todd wiped his beak on the branch removing the last of the drippy dead turtle.

"That seems like a fair price to pay for all that dead." Jack settled in sharing the tree branch with his best friend.

A morning roost before heading back to the main flock. They fell into a morning nap watching a handful of turkey vultures argue over a half eaten dead drippy turtle below. Vultures are the busboys of nature. Leave a mess. They take it away. Jack had never seen a vulture show up to the yellow house. His lady human was the busboy and server there. That didn't leave much for a vulture to do with their time.

Jack gazed below watching the father vulture teach his son how to bus a dead drippy turtle. There seemed to be a fair bit of talent required. The mother vulture stood to the side of the training area. She seemed less than interested in the turtle. Family is important. Family is important to a crow. Crows live under a strong sense of rules and regulations. Most any question a young crow can ask can be answered by consulting the Crow Code. A batch of laws taught and memorized by every crow before they fully fledge. One law held you don't leave a flock unless you intend to start your own. The only question unanswered in the Crow Code was the question; why? He'd asked this often of his parents. They replied simply, "Because you are a crow and that's how it's always been done."

The Crow Code also had crow suggestions. Expanded ideas to help make things easier. When one does leave ones' flock to create their own family it is expected you chose a tree within flight for your parents. So the grandparents can visit the grand crows, this suggestion came from his mother. Jack did not feel confident in asking why on that matter.

His drowsy thoughts were certain he was not ready for his own tree, wife, or kids. He hadn't even trained a human yet. He looked over at a sleeping Todd. He wasn't even sure if he could trust a dead turtle slurping best friend to help decide if his human was ready. He wasn't sure he could trust himself to decide what he wanted.

By all accounts in his own head, Jack was certain of nothing.

He slipped into sleep preparing himself for that inevitable flock interrogation that came next. He'd heard once that the humans call a flock of crows a murder. There were times he felt like he might.

*****

The swarm grew dense and raucous circling the top of Todd's pine tree. Each individual vying for a branch position. Inevitably the number of members caused moments of consternation between each other over locations and branches. Jack woke up in the din's middle. His family, extended family, and close friends were flying in for the afternoon foraging. A landing member's wing slapped him on the side of the head. It was Jerry

"HEY! Wake up Slumberjack! We're back!"

Jerry. Neither smooth with the ladies, nor concerned with the etiquette of greetings and slumbering friends. He'd claimed his permanent state of bachelorhood after the farmer's dinner incident. Which left Jerry with way too much time on the wing and a story of trees far away that overlooked a giraffe. Who according to Jerry, was a genius.

Todd, not having had his head slapped, opened one eye to give Jerry a quick once over. "Thanks for the heads-up Jer. I'm not sure we'd make it through the day without your hourly bulletins of obvious." Todd flapped his wings against himself to realign the few displaced with the incoming winds and wings.

It has been written in books by humans about birds, that flocking is the act of all participants in the flock agreeing on goals and supporting each other's efforts to same. This is a half truth. If you aren't a bird, and haven't been in a flock coming and going, you miss the the fine details of things. Things like two birds asleep on a branch, not being warned about the incoming remaining flock members. There hasn't been any agreeing to anything, because the lone two were asleep. You can't very well agree to anything while you are snoring.

When that agreeable flock shows up un-agreeably it's much more like a flood carrying away more water against it's will. The later being a quiet pool, nestled in a low lying sandy basin. Cool from the shade cast from a large tree and it's large leaves. Peaceful. Then the dam breaks and Jerry shows up. Nobody has written about that.

Jack took three side steps away from Jerry. He winced a little. Not from the pain of Jerry's landing. There wasn't any. But from the chaotic level of energy bursting off every square inch of Jerry. Jack felt like he needed to shield his eyes from all the mayhem in one bachelor crow. Potential carries weight forward into objects. Jerry was a living, breathing, potential boulder careening down a mountain, laughing.

"Jerry, what is your problem!? You did this yesterday! In fact, confronted with your redundant nature, you've been doing this for two years now."

Jerry laughed, crowed, and laughed again. "Jack my friend, you worry too much. Life's short. Get on with living it rather than the planning it." Jerry shoved his shoulder into Jack's for emphasis. A gusto delivered for exclamation as he tipped forward and flew straight down to the ground to begin the day's foraging travels. Over his shoulder he yelled back at Jack. "Stop thinking and fly Jack! What's the worst that could happen?"

Jack could hear his crow cackling as Jerry landed. "I could end up with drippy dead turtle for lunch, Jerry." He let his answer to Jerry float inside his own head. Sometimes talking with Jerry worked better as a monologue.

In the annals of wild things, the question, 'what's the worst that could happen?', had been answered. The short answer is, quite a lot actually. The long answer involved Dave and his human.

Dave had spent one full season training the human he named 'Seriously' to build fires. Throwing the flint rocks at the same time proved to be the most challenging. Once Seriously threw one rock into the forest before throwing the second at the mound of grass. Dave threw up his paws looking into the tall grass at the edge of the forest hoping to see some hint of where the flint had landed. "Seriously? This is your idea of throwing two rocks into the pile of sticks?" By the end of summer Seriously had created a leather pouch out of the rabbit he'd cooked for Dave on a Tuesday. He used it to carry his flint rocks wherever Dave and he wondered. Dave would find a stump or smooth rock to rest, letting Seriously know it was time to make a fire.

Dave spent all of the Fall weather training Seriously to hunt multiple wild things to eat. Weasels like having extra meal preparations at the ready. Additionally having a human also meant the wild things were bigger. He wasn't stuck eating a rat anymore. He could eat the good stuff, like deer. Fresh deer. Not leftover deer from a mountain lion that couldn't eat another mouthful.

By end of Fall, Seriously grew into a proper hunter-gatherer. This again was told by humans as some sort of domesticated wolf hunting with a human who trained it.

But anyone who was any wild thing knew it was Dave.

At the start of winter Dave and Seriously found themselves in a pickle. (Later that pickle would be referred to as the Ice Age.) Wild things were few and far between. The cave that Dave and Seriously inhabited offered protection from the ice aging and growing around them, but it did not provide the wild things to eat. Two carnivores, one trained one smarter, nibbled on smaller and smaller wild things. The fires Seriously started became smaller as well. No use is building a deer sized fire for a lizard meal.

One blustery winter afternoon a new human showed up at the cave. Much like the day Seriously appeared. This human was different and Dave could tell Seriously was excited. Dave let Seriously keep it. To his way of thinking what's one more human? Seriously could show this new human all the trainings he himself had had to show Seriously. To his way of thinking, Seriously could cut training time in half. Dave named this new human, 'What'. What quickly revealed a secret, she was a she, and Seriously was a he; Seriously…What's the worst that could happen.

The last chapter in the book of wild things states only a few facts. No one was there to witness the end of Dave and Seriously. Some say he died a peaceful death. Others postulate that once things got desperate, What decided a wandering weasel wasn't worth having under foot. And she took offense to a creature giving her orders. What took Seriously aside and made it clear it was the weasel or her.

Artifacts dug up later in a cave in upper Canada show a dinner was eaten at some point. Bones lay alongside a fire pit. The remains of two cave humans were also laid to rest not far off and out of the cave. A female human was found face down in what was once a river bed. Possible drowning. The male remains were found in such a way as to suggest he was stabbed with a burning stick, through the heart.

The story tells of a fight to the death. Dave dispatched What and Seriously, but not without injury. He drug his spent and injured body back to the cave next to the fire. There he ate left over lizard, warmed on a stone.

What was making dinner when she nodded to Seriously indicating the choice he had no choice to make. Their fight to the death began there. No matter the outcome, Dave had no intention of wasting a perfectly good left over lizard dinner.

*****

The full flock numbered in the hundreds. On hundred, seventy three specifically. Territory, resources, and parenting life cycles broke down that main number into multiple smaller flocks of hundreds. Divide those again for goals and personal preferences and a full main crow flock of 173 could become 10 groups of 17 each, plus scraggling extras. Jerry, Todd, and Jack made up that last bit.

Jack sustained himself on those breakaway periods. Family reunions were fine, but the barrage of questions about the future were exhausting. Jerry and Todd's questions were naturally rhetorical with little expectation. If they asked him about his human and how her training was going, they meant just that.

There was no underlying motivation to know if he was thinking of a specific girl crow, or if he had a mating date picked out. Was she learning or was she not, this lady human of his? He could or could not answer the question. Their question was friendly. With as much concern or weight as asking about the tidal creek's fish count. It was a simple question, and they could if they wanted to, find the answer out themselves.

Family questions were layered offerings that felt like traps waiting to be tripped. An accepted answer was rewarded with another question. An unaccepted answer was challenged with the same question asked a different way. In either case there were answers to tease out of his brain, or simply make up to appease the family member. He found himself confronted with just such a conversation over a bush full of berries. His second aunt on his father's side had joined him. She perched just above and in front of him.

"So. Jack. Your mother tells me you are training a human. The same lady human your father trained before you hatched! How exciting for you." Aunt Ellen hopped lower to find the next good berry.

"I wouldn't say I'm training the lady human yet. I feel she's remembering things dad taught her and, you know, trying it all again."

Aunt Ellen hopped again even further into the center of the bush. "Training humans is difficult. They seem to forget just about anything important. They remember everything that isn't important. And then do just the opposite of what you try to show them. I remember my first human training session. I was too young to understand their ways. I found the whole process trying at the beginning. At least you have your father's first trained. That should help you!"

Jack liked his Aunt Ellen. She was a positive thinker, and a good foraging partner. She always left the best bits behind for the next hunter. He supposed she did that because she wasn't concerned about how much she could gather, she was too busy focusing on what she had already.

Ellen as a young crow, learned the Crow Code well. She also ignored it well. Quietly. With no fuss given. She'd decided it was far more interesting to do the things others avoided. The excitement lay in knowing you did it and they didn't. Being a girl crow collecting experiences rather than attention, most other crow left her to her own devices. Better to watch someone make a mistake than partake in it yourself. Such was the Crow Code, and it's suggested addendum collection.

Ellen found her truth at the end of a hot summer. Humidity was the last to give up it's grip in the pine trees. September and October wrestled in the winds. Far off in the distance a farmer harvested corn from his fields. Her family would wait for him to collect the last of the corn, leaving harvested lines of picked over corn stalks. They gave the farmer a day past that, just in case he should return. Ellen thought it silly. Left over corn on the ground was dry and rodent molested. Ellen knew better than to think left behind corn was just as good as the corn still on the stalk. She made her decision that late afternoon while her murder waited at the edge of the farm where the soy beans grew. They all watched the dust rise from behind the tracker implement as the farmer followed planting lines harvesting his ready corn. Ellen broke rank and made flight to the corn field landing on a stalk behind the tractor that had already passed. He'd be back to gather up this line of corn, by the count in her head it would be long enough for her to dig her way through thick sweet corn husk to find the freshest corn kernels waiting. She had plenty of time to eat. She had plenty of corn to choose from.

When Ellen returned to the murder's pine tree all eyes were on her in shock, looking right at her. Who does such a thing as to break the Crow Code! Who would eat before the rest and in front of a harvesting farmer? The condemnation and jealousy of her fearlessness revealed to her the bare naked truth of the Crow Code. It was, at best, suggestions all. The Code made just enough sense to trap you, but not enough sense to free you. Her crop full and her mindful ideas confirmed, Ellen became a whole new crow that day.

"Aunt Ellen, can I ask you a personal question?" Jack hopped to the top branch of the heavier fruited side.

"Of course you can Jack." She smiled over her shoulder and hopped further down.

"Did you ever think maybe you wouldn't, you know, make a family? Maybe you thought you were meant to do something else first. Or maybe..." Jack looked through the branches and into the sky above. "maybe you didn't know what to do, but you felt that what everyone expected wasn't it anyway?"

He watched his Aunt stop hunting and perch. She gave his question a good long thought. Her answers were always at the end of good long thoughts. She gave herself and Jack a thoughtful shrug.

"Jack, the only thing I've ever known is how to be a crow like all the other crows I know, unless of course they are making no sense with all their doings. Now maybe that is an excuse not to be a crow, or maybe that is a superb reason to be a me. I'm not sure." Aunt Ellen moved to the next fine berry.

Jack laughed inside, she was so honest in all she did. "I was just thinking maybe I should try being just me and being good at that first before, you know, finding the tree, finding the girl, and being a dad to the hatchling part, and all that Crow Code to follow."

"I don't see how that would be a wrong idea Jack. But how will you know you are a good you? When will you know you're done doing that?" Aunt Ellen looked at Jack with a genuine curiosity. Her nephew was always thinking so deeply. She found it disconcerting and genuine just like she found it in her brother, Jack's Dad.

"I don't know Aunt Ellen. But maybe if I don't know, I really can't know anything else. Maybe knowing isn't so much being good at what's expected, but being good at choosing other things and just trying." They looked into the sky pondering this last thought together.

"One other thing I know. The one thing I believe can be known, Jack. When we stop asking questions that's when we stop knowing. Trying sounds about the same as asking questions." Neither had another answer to give, they offered each other their company inside that moment of mystery.

*****

The sun shimmered through the oak trees on the other side of the creek. Jack had long ago bid farewells and see you soon to his Aunt. He found himself alone again, on a table at the yellow house. Jack peered into the window looking for his lady human. All he saw was a big blue parrot staring back. Parrot faces were funny looking no matter what they were doing with them.

Jack met a parrot once. On a wire. He had escaped his cage and was free. At least that's how Jack saw it.

He spotted the red parrot from quite a distance away. It was impossible to miss all that red. Jack flew in to perch on the same wire to get a closer look. He'd never seen a red bird that big before. Its feet were enormous. How did this bird get those big feet wrapped around a wire? He had to know how those big scaly feet worked around a skinny wire.

"Hey! I'm Jack Crow." He'd perched close enough to talk, if the red parrot wanted to talk. He didn't seem that interested though. Whatever, Jack thought. I'll just sit here and observe this guy for a while. Jack acted like he was going for a nap, one eye open. He kept both eyes open but red parrot couldn't see the other one. Jack observed under camouflage of napping. Time passed.

"What do you think you're looking at?" Red parrot asked directly from the center of their shared silence.

"I'm not looking, I'm napping. Been a long morning. Just trying to catch a few Zs." Jack looked away and down to the ground shrugging, as if to prove his lack of interest in a very interesting red parrot.

"Sure. You don't live in a cage in a house and not know when someone is looking at you when they are pretending not to look at you." Red parrot shifted on the wire turning his head toward Jack. Jack stared at a beak that was the size of a pinecone.

"Um. Sorry. It's hard not to want to meet a fellow like you. I mean. You are red. And huge. And your feet are huge. And your beak is huge. And your..." the parrot interrupted Jack's rambling.

"I get the picture small fry." Red parrot shifted again to look the other way. He'd had this same conversation the day before, with a mockingbird. He'd hoped to keep this from becoming some sort of habit in the wildverse.

"Oh, I didn't mean to insult, I was..."

"Yeah. You were. But let's pretend I'm bored. What's your name? And what are you small fry?" Red parrot turned his attention back to Jack.

"My name is Jack. I'm a crow. What's your name?"

"They call me Crackers. I'm a Greenwing Macaw. But as you can see my wings are not all green. So leave it to a human to get that wrong, too." Crackers laughed at his own joke.

"HA! Humans!" Best Jack could do at this point is follow Crackers' lead on matters of opinion, subject, and when to laugh.

Crackers and he talked until the sun touched the rooftops. It was obvious Crackers didn't mind being free. He wasn't afraid of anything. He was too big. He figured out where the bird baths and good water was for a few miles. Fruit trees, palm trees and a couple local gardens supplied enough food for 30 parrots. And he made friends with a dog name Barney, two streets down. Barney got delicious leftovers occasionally. Living the wild side was all right with Crackers.

Jack told Crackers about being a crow. Family, commitments, making hatchlings, training humans, and such.

"Wow Jack. It's almost like you're in a cage, without a cage." Crackers settled his beak into his shoulder feathers. He'd learned all he wanted to know. Now he needed a nap.

Jack didn't need a nap. He needed to revisit this training issue at the yellow house. He needed to know what he didn't know. He perched quietly, a bit disappointed he hadn't gotten around to understanding how a big red bird gets his big red bird feet wrapped around a little wire, and left the regret behind as he took flight to the yellow house.

*****

"HI!" A sung greetings, followed by what Jack could only describe as tree shaking guttural shrieks, rattled the porch. The parrot in the yellow house was making no sense louder than most nonsensical folk.

"HEY!" Jack called back. Better keep it simple until he figured out if this one was as smart as Crackers.

"What are you doing on my thing? Who are you? I saw you the other day. You didn't share your food. Why are you on my thing and not sharing food? That seems rude." Jack stopped dead in his thoughts. Okay, this one is a girl.

"Oh, hey. Sorry about not sharing. I thought you would automatically get some since you live here. I'm Jack Crow."

"Oh. Okay I'm Butters. And you should know I didn't get any of whatever you got. Which I doubt you can fix, anyway. You are out there on my thing and I'm in here. You are tiny. Does that bother you? It would bother me if I was small. But I'm not. I'm big and blue and beautiful. Mom told me I was.

So I must be. She said you were interesting. Small and interesting." Butters continued to mumble about sea shells and other small and interesting things while fussing with her wing feathers.

"Okay. Good to know. Hey Butters, is she in there?" Jack wanted to get to the point. The day was ending, and night was starting soon.

Points to consider when wanting to live with a parrot should be inserted here. Because most people when given the chance would entertain the idea. Parrots are intriguing. And interesting. Macaws are all that and will take advantage of being ultra cute with a side of vocabulary to keep their humans in line. Butters being a Blue and Gold Macaw, specifically of the Bolivian line, is lazy. She would prefer nothing more than to lazily go through her day. Jack Crow has plans and goals. Butters has no plans and one goal. Napping. Sharing a house with a parrot is similar to sharing your house with a child. A child that is smarter than you, has no concerns about priority or propriety and will execute an idea before it's fully bloomed in their head. Keeping up with a parrot is work. Additionally their face comes with industrial clamping snips. Your furniture will never win an argument with a parrot.

"Is who in here?"

"The lady who says you are big and blue and beautiful. And I am interesting." He waited wondering if he'd have to decelerate the conversation. Butters was either slow, or didn't care to go fast.

"OH! Mom's in the upstairs doing whatever is up there." Butters looked away from Jack and toward what Jack assumed were "stairs".

She did not look back at Jack but rather gazed while sticking a talon into her nose. Jack was going to have to work intently on keeping this bird's attention.

"She's your ...mom?" Jack paused. Moms lay eggs. That's how that worked and he could not picture the lady human laying eggs in a nest. Not at all.

"What? NO! Are you slow or something!?" Butters stopped preening and looked at Jack through the window. And spoke ever so slowly. This crow bird was obviously challenged. "I call her Mom, because she likes it. She likes being the mom in here and taking care of every other body like a mom. I call her Mom to make her feel good. Because she is very nice and so that seems fair." Butters waited and looked at Jack for some sign of comprehension.

"Oh. Yeah, sure. I get it. Should I call her mom? Since she's been nice to me?"

"What? She doesn't speak Crow! She won't understand a word you're saying." With that Butters took flight off the cage door and toward the direction of the upstairs.

Jack perched on the table's edge working through this new information. Mom, but not a mom, but call her a mom but not if you only speak Crow. He did not understand how his father trained this lady human. He was pulled from his thoughts by a voice through the glass. "Hi Jack!"

"I forgot the sea shells!" Jack jumped from the table into the bowl of seashells and dug. She laughed.

Just one more thing he probably wouldn't understand. As quickly as possible Jack dug, throwing the wrong shells aside, trying to find the right shells.

He looked up in between tosses. She'd left. He stopped his mad dash of digging and sighed. "I should have gone to the shells and bypassed the Butters."

He flew to the top of the fence nearby. Go home, or forage somewhere else? He pondered the options. Until a door opened. Lady human came out onto the deck and laid things out on the table. Jack was shocked. Flabbergasted even. Why he hadn't even paid for this, nor ordered anything!? He just showed up. He just showed up, waited, talked to a Butters and then there was food. Can just showing up deliver a message? Is there value to a human for just being available? Were they that easy to please? And now he felt guilty. He'd have to bring something next time. Something unusual and quite special. Positive reinforcement level something.

"Jack come off the fence, I've got apple slices, blueberries, and a slice of cheese. Eat what you like, I'm sure the squirrels will take what you leave." With that she turned around and went back into her house. She didn't even stay by the window to watch. She left him a dinner without a fuss.

He flew back to the table to inspect dinner bits. Two squirrels were in the grass in front of the deck, conspiring. Squirrels. It's not that crows dislike squirrels. Crows, including Jack, just do not appreciate their unwillingness to share or cooperate. To a crow's way of thinking it isn't difficult to discuss divvying up dinners and then sticking to the plan. To a squirrel's way of thinking, it's difficult and unnecessary. The last squirrel agreement Jack entered into went sideways as quickly as the squirrel had agreed to his terms.

"Okay squirrel, we both want some of this tasty cantaloupe right?" Jack stood on the ground in front of the squirrel and behind the cantaloupe they both found at they same time.

He thought he'd gotten up early enough to beat this guy to the Sunday Market fruit selling place. But, squirrel tried the same tactic. Getting up early to beat Jack.

Getting up early wasn't the solution to the situation. Squirrels get up early on principle. Most wild things do. Getting to where you are going alone is the solution. The Sunday Market had grown over the years. There were 38 different vendors plying their wares. Everything from food to musical instruments to a woman who created furniture out of discarded linoleum. With 38 vendors, 23 of them being farmers, the local wild things faired well. Add in benches with seated snacking humans, most wild things had their fill by the time the market closed. The situation for Jack and Squirrel boiled down to the fact that this particular vendor was the only one who had cantaloupes. There were watermelon vendors, and a few squash and oranges vendors. There were also 4 vendors fighting for customers interested in dragon fruits. But only one cantaloupe vendor located at the outside vendor setup, closest to the park. Crows and squirrels saw it all unfold from the trees above. There was bound to be moments of discord. Which simply required agreements and protocols agreed upon. One would think. And if one did think, then one was not a squirrel.

"Yeah. Yayayaya, right. I want that." Squirrel rolled his hands over and over, looking back and forth and back at Jack.

"Okay, so since we both want this, we should split it evenly and we each get a fair share." Jack looked into the squirrel's eyes, to see if any of this registered with the twitchy guy.

"Yeah. Yayayayaya, right!" Squirrel rolled his hands over and over, nodding his head and looking back and forth and back at Jack. And then he twitched his whiskered nose.

And on any other given day, not this early, Jack would have caught that sign. He would have seen the conspiracy a million feet away. But it was early, and he was focused on keeping the fruit near and the squirrel agreeing.

"So we agree I will split this in half and you keep one half and I keep the other half. I'll even let you choose which half you want. My beak is sharp. You have little hands, so I'm probably better for this part of the agreement." Jack squinted his eyes and looked closely at squirrel's to see where the deal was going.

"Yeah. Yayayayayayaya, right!" Squirrel jumped straight up and a second squirrel ran right under Jack grabbing the cantaloupe chunk and literally disappeared before the deal breaking squirrel hit the ground again. He never landed either, it was more like he bounced himself into the same direction and disappeared. Laughing. Loudly.

Jack looked into the windows one more time checking for lady human. He shook off the anxiety of a dirty squirrel deal gone bad before realizing the current squirrel threat had squirmed under the fence and away. Jack ate one blueberry on the table and then flew out with an apple chunk. He landed on the fence top to eat and observe. Were the dastardly untrustworthy twitchy squirrels coming back, or were they not? And why did she not need an order or payment? So many questions needing answers. But the apple was sweet, no question about that.

*****

Jack woke in the family tree, with Todd perched near and one branch up.

"Hey! Slumberjack, you awake yet or what?" Things to do, trees to view. Todd was just about over all this sleeping in the family tree business. And he'd just as soon find his own and pretend to find a wife. Not that the wife idea was a bad idea, but wives led to nests. And that adds up to work. Not that the work idea was a bad idea. He'd just prefer to not do that kind of work, yet.

"Slumberjack!" Todd dropped an oak branch on Jack's head for affect.

"Seriously? I heard you the first time." Jack rustled and shifted his weight.

"Then why didn't you answer ssslummmberjack?" The nickname was more annoying drawn out. And Todd knew it.

"Because I intended on ignoring you until the sun came up. Sunrise. You've heard of that right?" Jack refused to open his eyes. What you can't see will eventually disappear. He hoped.

"Sunrise!? SUNrise? Jack I've got important business to attend to and you are my right-hand bird! I need your opinion on matters of grave consideration." Todd hopped down to Jack's branch, for better badgering.

"Todd I told you already, just pick a tree. If it's close enough to make your mom happy, but far enough to keep her from visiting easily. It's the right tree. We live in a forest of trees! Trees are everywhere. Just choose one." Jack opened his eyes on that last statement for affect. "And then invite me over for the tree claiming."

"Jack I'll make you a deal. You help me choose a tree. And I'll help you decide if that lady human you talk about is worth training. How about that?"

Jack held a skeptical eye toward Todd. He'd been feeling confident in his human, slightly cautious, but confident. Twice now she'd brought food simply for showing up. The question was; is he training her or is she training him? Jack wasn't certain at all about involving Todd in discovering the answer. If they found by reasoning he was being trained by her, then Jack would never hear the end of that at any foraging lunch. Conversely, if they found by reasoning he was training her and so well that she brought foods out for showing up, Todd did not need to know about any of that.

It's well known in the world of Crow that humans make excellent partners in life needs. They are trainable; they are friendly mostly, and they have all kinds of tasty foods. Humans come in handy. They don't require large doses of maintenance or time. Bring a rock, get a meal. And if you've worked your training right, you don't even need the rock. Or in Jack's case, just show up. But there is a point where humans fall apart. Crows call it the 'Hitchcock Affect'. Actually one crow called it that, explained it to other crows and over time it theory was proven right.

Morty got caught up with training one of his humans late into the day, as the story goes. Long ago, a few generations back, Morty the Crow found his trainable human near a tree that had a yard that had a house next to it. Every day at 4 in the afternoon his human brought out a plate of tastes and sat in a chair under the tree in the yard by the house. It was expected that Morty perch in the tree, closest branch to the chair and share. Much like Jack's human all Morty had to do was show up and crow call.

One late into the day, his human did something different. His human brought out a table. He brought out foods to his table. His human would hand him a piece of whatever the taste with every plate he set at the table.

Then his human had more humans show up and help bring out more tables and more foods. He stayed in his tree watching, mostly because his human would bring something over to a branch and leave it for him. The sharing was the same, the time began to go longer, but all in all it was the same to the human. It was important to his human he eat everything offered. Morty felt compelled to hang out and eat while observing the way of a horde of human. That's what crows call groups of humans. A Horde. A group of humans dancing is a Horde of Convulsion.

The day became dusk, and the humans ate while a movie showed on a sheet hung from his tree. The movie was shocking. The movie was insulting. The movie got it all wrong. Morty could not believe his eyes. Crows were attacking people in the street and the humans were cheering and laughing and telling the killer crows in the movie to do it again. One human said to another human, "Hitchcock was a genius. One bird is great, but put them in a group and they are awful! This is the best horror movie ever."

Morty looked at the screen. Then back to the talking humans. Back at the screen. Hitchcock. That human says one bird is good, a group is awful. He flew to his family tree to discuss this information. After a family meeting, it was decided crows would not Hitchcock at the beginning of training stages. First one crow will train one human and earn their trust. After some time, he would bring a friend for introductions. If the second friend is accepted, then family and friends could join in the visits. Slowly at first as not to Hitchcock the trained human. This plan has worked for generations and has even been fine tuned to meet local customs.

For instance, humans with fences tend not to mind a murder of crow. Humans without fences do because that's a large number of crow on their grass.

They care about their grass. If they have a fence a crow and his family can stay off the grass. This seems to help the human accept their place and position. Fences also give a crow better viewing to see where the foods may be waiting. Because of Morty's work and sacrifice all crows have a fine tuned approach to the human needing training.

Jack regarded Todd, considered Morty and found the answer to his problem of trees, wives, and hatchlings. He'd Hitchcock his lady human! Which would reset expectations and give him time to find out what he didn't know! This was genius and should probably be added to the Crow Code one day.

"Todd let's work on finding you that perfect tree. After breakfast. I'm starving." Jack flew off his branch with new energy. He had a plan if need be. That felt good. Todd followed and caught up in midair flight.

"Hey, let's go back to the place I found the turtle egg, Jack!" Todd grinned and soared. "Maybe there'll be two, one each!" And with that Todd laughed all the way to where he found that turtle egg.

*****

The view was impressive. Jack had to admit that to Todd. The neighborhood looked promising for training and it was the perfect distance from family and flock, close enough, but not too close. "Do you have a human picked out around here yet?" Jack looked over his shoulder to hear Todd's answer. Todd was finishing up the turtle egg he'd brought from the breakfast site.

"Not yet." He swallowed and looked around his possible new world. "But there's got to be one good trainable human in the middle of all this possible."

"Well, I vote this tree." Jack looked down between branches to appreciate the height of the oak tree. "Oaks are great family trees if you ask me. And you did."

"Speaking of a family, let's go visit that human of your dad's that you're retraining for yourself."

"You want to go over there and see the place or are you wanting to see what she brings out?" Todd constantly ate, even when he wasn't hungry. Operation Hitchcock may as well get underway.

"That depends on how inspired your human is to impress us. If it's good eats, I'm eating."

Jack led the way to the yellow house next to the creek that fed a lake across the way. That was the best part of the yellow house. The lady human was a second best to go along with it.

Jack and Todd landed on the fence belonging to the yellow house.

"Whoa. Nice! A fence, too!" Todd took in the scene sincerely impressed. There were ibis, ducks, blue jays (Todd hated those guys) and squirrels running around. And they were all eating something at the same time. This place was practically a restaurant! "Jack, I think you have your human, and your tree." Todd nodded behind them at a 35 foot pine tree directly behind the yellow house and its backyard buffet.

Jack cringed. That tree was perfect. And perfectly not what he has in mind right now. Yes. The place was perfect. A creek, a lake, a house, a semi-trained human, and the tree. Yup. It was a perfect setup for exploring nothing, if you wanted to avoid such things.

Which Jack did not want to avoid. It felt substantial and wrong to avoid the things you don't know. Jack did not know so many things.

"That tree was your Dad's tree, you should just go get it right now." Todd turned around on the fence to look up at Edgar's first tree ever. "Everybody knows about that tree. I'm surprised you are just now setting all this up. Didn't your Dad already introduce you and get you a head start?"

"Yeah, last year. I've been procrastinating." Which wasn't a lie in the strictest sense, but he left out details about their tree argument. When thinking on it now, here with Todd, it wasn't an argument about a tree. It was an argument about Jack being like his dad and like every other crow. And that his dad just set all this up assuming he'd take it over and take a next step that no one even asked him about in the first place. He hadn't even finished fledging when his Dad brought it up. Granted, his father left him to his own the following week, but that makes no difference.

"Jack I want you to know this is all yours." his father began. "I spent quite a bit of time working with the lady human in the yellow house. She's smart. And that tree, is yours. And this backyard is yours, but I recommend just hopping on that deck, it's shaded. There's the creek and the lake if she's not around for other eating. I think you can make a nice family life here. You know your mother and I did." Edgar looked down from the small crepe myrtle tree watching his son beg for a meal. They grow up so fast, he thought. First, they can barely fly, and then they are fully capable and refusing to accept that fact. Edgar sighed.

"Dad! I'm hungry!" Jack called with his mouth wide open waiting.

"Son. You don't need me. You think you do. Now look down and forage like I showed you." Edgar patiently waited and thought on the last few years he and Helen had invested in this place. Helen liked the tree here better than their current, but sometimes you have to make changes. The turkey vultures weren't cooperating as much this year. Sharing is a two way street, or a clogged cul-de-sac depending on the cooperation.

"DAD! I can't do it!" Jack hunkered closer to the ground in an effort to look needy and miserable. "Com'on Dad!"

"Son, there's everything you need. Eat. I'll get dinner for you later. Now, you get your own lunch."

Jack called out in frustration and stood up. This wasn't working out as he'd thought. What was all this about his tree, his lake, his creek, his human? None of that has to do with him, anyway. He picked through some leftovers from a lunch lady human had served earlier to the local ducks. He didn't mind popcorn at all. But he minded having to get it himself. He wasn't ready for all this yet. He didn't even know who he was and what he wanted. Outside of lunch being brought to him.

He stopped foraging for a moment and looked up into the tree his father perched himself in. "What am I supposed to do with a tree and a lake and a creek and a lady human in this house, anyway?" Jack waited for an answer to his future.

His father laughed. "Why, you start a family son! Not right now, but soon enough."

Jack looked up at his father and asked, "How soon is soon enough?"

His father never answered that question. He'd asked it of him a few more times, and once last week to no avail. Edgar would look at him and smile. When a father just looks at you and smiles it's not that they have secret knowledge. It's more like they are trying to keep the fact they don't have an answer, secret. So there was no answer. And if there's no answer, there's no real question. And if there's no question then he sure doesn't have to do anything related to this idea of trees and families soon. And that worked for a few seasons.

Todd has a point. If he didn't make some proactive moves to show his parents he was serious about one day doing something maybe, things could get awkward at dinner.

"Yeah, I should make that move soon. So, what about the house? What do you think about all this?" Jack watched Todd fly over to the deck and perch on a chair. "What the crow, Todd!? You'll confuse her!" But before Jack could fly in and straighten out the Todd problem, his lady human walked out onto the deck.

"Hi crow!" She smiled and looked at Todd. "Where's Jack?"

Jack took his cue and flew in to land opposite Todd on another chair. He called to make sure she noticed. Muddled humans can be difficult to un-muddle.

"Hi Jack! I'm happy to see you again. So, you brought a friend? That's nice."

Lady human looked back to Todd. "I'll call you... Barbossa. Since you are a friend of Jack's, but I think you'd take his ship." She laughed as she went back into the house.

"Now what Jack? She didn't even bring anything." Todd looked around in shock. Edgar didn't train this human well at all! He perched unimpressed and unfed.

"I dunno Barbossa, let's wait and see." Jack laughed a crow cackle and relaxed knowing he was on the correct table, and she had the right idea bout Todd.

Todd called out a sharp rebuke. "Not funny Jack! How about I have my human call you Shirley?"

"You'll need a trained human first Todd." Jack hopped to the furthest side of the table, leaving room for her to serve lunch, not concerned about who was training who in all this because at this point it didn't matter. Like being right in an argument when the result will be the same for both crows. Todd was busy picking around the seashells in the pot, "So these are the shells you don't even have to hunt for ...and she still sees them as payment? Wow."

As he dropped a shell from the pot onto the table in front of Jack as an example, lady human came outside through her door carrying lunch. She smiled. Jack liked that part about her. Smiling goes a long way. Jerry smiles but his is a smile you knew only brought chaos. This smile she wore, was one that said, "we're friends". As much as a human and a crow could be friends. No crow had ever broached that subject. It seemed to Jack, particularly today, that it could be possible.

"All right boys, I made little crow sized peanut butter and jelly sandwiches, cut a few grapes in half, and shelled walnuts. Hopefully, you like all my ideas."

Then she did a thing that took Jack by surprise. She laid everything out in two sets, each with the same count of things. And she did it on the other table.

"I don't want you fighting over food, and I don't want to scare you by getting too close, so... here you go!"

And with that flurry of presentation, lady human went back into the yellow house through the windowed door. Jack could see Butters perched on her cage watching. And again, lady human did the most amazing thing as she walked in her house. She handed crow sandwiches to Butters, and the other birds he'd not yet met, but lived in the house as well. She walked up to every bird, spoke words and handed them their portions with her smile. And each bird took the portion straight from her hand. Without hesitation. Without pause. Without a second thought of not doing it. Butters held her peanut butter and jelly sandwich in her talons, balanced on her other foot on the door of her cage and looked right at Jack. He heard her laugh while giving her portion her full attention.

"Whoa." Todd was dumbstruck. "If you don't claim that tree and this human, you, my friend are lost in all things crow." He hopped over to the table to grab his share of the foods. "And I don't mind telling you this looks delicious!" He grabbed a grape. "It's still cold!" He dived into the crow-sized sandwich of peanut butter and jelly. "Blackberry jelly!? Jack, you are not good enough for this place."

"Shut it Barbossa." Jack followed Todd's lead and joined him on the larger table for lunch. Neither thought about grabbing and going like normal.

"Jack you can call me anything you like as long as I'm eating here when you do it." Todd laughed with his mouth full. Jack joined him. And the lady in the house laughed quietly not knowing exactly what these two crows were saying to each other, but offered a good guess to the universe.

Todd finished first as Jack worked on the last bit of walnuts. "HEY! Let's go get your tree at least. I mean ...we're here."

Jack thought about it. It couldn't hurt, and it's not like he has to do all that wife and hatchling thing right away. But it would be foolish to not grab the tree. Because for a crow, that's also grabbing this lady human and her yellow house. "You're right, I should claim that tree now."

*****

Claiming a tree is a big deal done quietly among crow. One male crow brings a few friends to a tree and shows them his choice. Unless one of his friends disagrees or says he wants it, you spend a few minutes jumping from branch to branch crowing about it. Crows like things simple and clear. No need muddying the waters with all kinds of unnecessary goings and comings.

"I should get Dad for this first." Jack looked into the yellow house once more and then at Todd.

"Yeah, let's go get him and then we can get that tree. I mean, you can get that tree. I should probably come over for dinner later to celebrate." And with that they both flew off in a flurry of feathers and laughter to search out the current owner of this yellow house, this lady human, and the pine tree across the way, Edgar Crow.

Inside the yellow house lady human, known as Lisa Douglas to other humans, watched Todd and Jack fly off into the sky calling to each other. She liked crows. She liked animals of all shapes and sizes, really. Animals are more sensible than humans. And frankly, they are more honest.

She preferred these times of service and visits with all the wildlife to time and service with humans. There's a quiet joy in being allowed inside the life moment of a wild creature. Being welcomed in and tested to see one's worth. Wildlife is fine tuned to reject lies and fiddling about. They have neither the time nor life to gamble with it. If a crow accepts your offers, seeks your attention, and then shares his or her space with you, it's safe to say you are doing all right as a human.

She'd created a friendship with a black bird when she was young. In Illinois black birds were considered nothing special at all. No matter where you looked you would see a flock of them. Her little home town was nestled in the center of northern Illinois corn and soy farmers. Food for black birds and other song singing fliers was everywhere. Which allowed them to choose anywhere. One summer day, one black bird made her backyard his anywhere.

He would perch on the stockade fence near their pool waiting on her. She would sneak the best of the garden's snap peas and lay them in a row on the top rail of the fence so he might have his fill. He would gladly share his space and time while eating with her. His deep black eyes said more than any one human has spoken in her entire life. Later when she returned to the backyard to play she would find his thank you on the fence. Yarn, a stone, sometimes a glass piece worn down in the slow moving creek nearby. They were his tokens of thanks, and her treasures to keep. It was then the idea began to birth into a certainty. Little things are important. Little things found anywhere are important. Being kind is most important of all.

She found herself in those summer days running home, or not leaving home at all to wait for her visitor and friend. She found herself happier for doing so.

Lisa's gaze moved from the empty deck to the area under the crepe myrtle just beyond. A familiar group of Muscovy ducks were foraging and drinking from the water bowls she left out for them and any other passersby. Her ducks were also an acid test to her own kindness. She supposed referring to wild ducks as "hers" was a stretch. But there too shown her weakness as a human, wanting to take ownership, or control if the ownership evaded. And yet for Lisa, "hers" meant she accepted an emotional attachment and promise to these waddling behemoth of the duck world. She never tried to catch one, she's never tried to coerce their eating or staying. Although she did once collect 2 ducklings after a fierce rainstorm. They were separated from their mother and family during the windswept rains. They only needed to spend one night with her as in the morning she could reunite one baby with his family. Hearing his brothers and sisters call out to him and run to gather him back was a satisfying moment. The second duckling did not survive the evening. Severely injured, his chances were slim from the moment she collected him from the ground. After delivering the healthy baby back to his flock, she sat on the deck with the duckling that would not make it further. Wrapped in a cloth she told him of the rising sun and his flock's foraging. She spoke softly and hoped to impart one last comforting sound as he left the living.

Death left no room for negotiations. Every creature has an ending. Every life will breathe and then cease that breath. She looked upon the duckling now gone and thought, no one should die alone. Lisa lay him gently on the ground next to the garden, still wrapped in a soft cloth. She carefully dug a perfectly sized grave for her charge. Her thoughts of love and thanks to him for allowing her to carry him to that last moment. Lisa ended that day thinking on the chasm of emotions one sunrise and sunset can bring if you pay attention to the little things.

Lisa stepped back onto the deck to watch her remaining ducklings chase bugs under the tree. She wanted to clean the table and inspect the crow leftovers. Like her parrots, if it's left behind or on the floor, that's a vote of no confidence. She'd soon learned that crows are far less picky about foods and food choices than a parrot. But then parrots keep their humans busy. Crows seemed more interested in keeping a schedule.

Edgar perched on top of the electrical pole looking into the distance. He'd need to be getting home soon. Helen had little patience with his meandering and wandering too long. He could make out the water of the Gulf of Mexico on the horizon. He could smell the salt air. And he thought about that great restaurant that left their garbage can open. That was a great place to find. One of his adventures that allowed him to share a great meal of fish and fries. He felt compelled to show her why he wondered. Why he felt compelled to make sure he'd not missed anything by being a crow. He wrestled with that fear of missing something. You stick too close to a schedule, and you might miss something. Like fish and fries.

"Dad!" Jack called out as he and Todd made progress through a head wind off the coastal waters. Afternoon wind changes brought salty smells and extra flying work. Todd flew behind him to catch a break from Jack's drift.

"Dad!"

Edgar turned around on his electrical pole and saw his son coming. "Jack!" He called twice, which is crow speak for a big hello and I love you, too. He called out to Todd. And smiled. His son and Todd had been inseparable since day one. He wondered where Jerry was, but dismissed the thought knowing Jack himself wouldn't have bothered wondering. Jerry was being Jerry and would show up when he finished being Jerry.

Jack lighted on the power line connected to the top of Edgar's pole. Todd came in fast and lighted on the power line below Jack's.

Jack settled his feathers and wings and smiled for his father. "Dad, I was going to claim your tree today, over at the yellow house. I'd like it if you would come and be there with me."

"And may I say Edgar, your lady human over in the yellow house is very well trained!" Todd nodded toward Edgar with respect.

"I appreciate that Todd, but I think her training started with her parrots, I had the luck to add crow to it." Edgar looked up to meet his son's eyes. "And I would be honored to help you claim the tree your mother and I so very much loved. Let's go!"

The three flew back to the pine tree near the yellow house with ease. The head wind was now a tail wind, and every crow loved those. Finding the pine tree was as simple as following the smells, the breeze and the water paths. From above, the world is a patchwork of colors, lines, and shady spots. The curve of the earth and the location of the sun tell stories in shadows and shade. From above, the world is a moving ever-changing pattern of paths and ways. Trees and water created avenues and lanes. A good crow would plan a trip based on all the trees and who had claimed them. One could visit as many relatives as one wanted in a simple trip to a favorite foraging spot. A crow choosing a tree kept that idea in mind.

A good tree, not only stood near moving water, but across from a faithful human if you were lucky. A good tree, offered height and width to accommodate a family, visitors, and the occasional stranger who needed a rest.

Unlike those mockingbirds, crows had no problem leaving space for others. And they left a fair amount of space. It was good to be a good neighbor. To a crow being a good neighbor was akin to being a good crow. There was plenty for all if all had the ability to access the plenty. There was room in everyone's life for kindness.

Edgar called out first, "There it is!" He banked left hard and swooped into the top third of the tree branches to disappear among them. Jack called and winked at Todd.

"After you Barbossa!" Jack offered with a laugh.

"Oh NO. After you Slumberjack!" They both banked left hard at the same time laughing at the winds.

*****

"I love this tree Jack. Your mother will be so pleased you've chosen it." Edgar looked around at the full healthy needles on the pine. It was taller than his last time here, and full of cones. It smelled good.

A voice came from a dark corner of a larger branch growing from the trunk below. "How long do you think you'll be here bothering me?"

Jack laughed, Todd joined in with an agreeable giggle. "We just now arrived and we're already a bother to you?" Jack liked a good question that already had an answer.

"You bothered me before you even showed up. That is why I was here first and not busy bothering you where you were before you came here!" The voice replied.

Edgar decided he would leave the negotiations to his son. It was a rite of passage, he too had his own voice to deal with oh so long ago. Edgar nestled onto his legs and took a comfortable grip on his branch. No matter how this turned out, it would be entertaining.

"It would be helpful to know who I am bothering. After all how do I know it really bothers you at all if I don't know who you are?" Jack put on his best adult voice and serious nature type crow speak.

"How do you know I am really bothered at all if ....what are you dribbling on about? That whole statement shows you for the lost soul of a crow you are. I am bothered because I told you I was bothered!" The voice rustled in the needles. "I am so bothered I may just leave this tree!"

An offer at last. These things can go on for a fair amount of time, you could never know just how long it would take to get an offer. And the first one to make an offer is usually the one that accepts the counteroffer. You need to hold out for that bit to claim a tree. Edgar grinned under his wing, pretending to nap, but all the while listening in.

Todd elbowed Jack. "It's the offer! Counter it!" Todd loved these tree negotiations. He would accept anyone's invitation to join in a tree claiming. The negotiations were hilarious!

Edgar waited. Todd snickered. Jack, had plans. He wanted his negotiations to be the best crow claim negotiations ever made. To tree claim well, a crow does not want to alienate those already in the tree. A great negotiation leads to everyone staying, sharing, and caring for a great tree. And a great crow is a great neighbor. He would do his best at this for a good story and a proud father.

"I wouldn't want you to leave this tree. I find your company pleasant. Maybe there is something I can do that would alleviate the bother for you?" His counter offer floated in the air. Todd waited silently. Edgar knew his son had already solved the negotiation.

"Well, I didn't say I WOULD leave, I said I MAY leave." The voice spoke plainly.

"That's true! I'm glad for it. Maybe we should start with introductions. I am Jack Crow, this is my friend Todd and my father Edgar. I'm pleased to meet you." The trio of crow waited for an answer.

From between the dark green pine needles and the long drooping branches that held them shown an eye. The eye looked up to Jack, over to Todd and around to Edgar, and returned its gaze to Jack. "Hello to you all. I am Stiltz. And this is Stretch, Ginger, Fred, Harvey, Jane, Tony, Shirley, Gary, Ralph, Shorty, Stubby, and Lenny."

Todd looked over at Jack with an incredulous shrug. If there were 12 others of this one, so be it. But he couldn't see them. Jack looked to his father for reassurance. Negotiating with one individual was one thing, but 12 others could get tricky. Edgar could only offer a fatherly smile of assurance mixed with "you're on your own son".

Jack looked back to the eye with a voice. "So, you've your flock with you. That's great! I can't see you though, not all of you or all of you all. It would sure help if I could see you, not necessarily all of you although." The pine needles rustled and parted like a curtain to reveal an Ibis.

"Oh! Nice to see you Stiltz Ibis." Jack relaxed.

Negotiating with Ibis was simply a task of acknowledgement. They spend little time in a tree. But will show up all together if the weather or the other ground creatures make it necessary. And thankfully they don't nest this far from the salt waters.

"And you too, Jack Crow. I remember you, over there. We met in this tree seasons ago. Edgar, right?" Stiltz leaned forward to take a better look.

"That's right. I had my wife Helen, with me. We came in to claim the tree. This is my son, Jack, we're back to claim the tree for him."

"AH! Well that's grand. Have you visited lady human in the yellow house lately? She's taken to offering shelter and foods to the ducks now. Me and mine go over all the time for eating." Stiltz Ibis rustled his feathers, which led a wave of honks and rustling from within the pine tree. More eyes revealed themselves between branches and pine needles.

"We plan on dropping in after claiming this tree, actually. It's been a while since I've been here." Edgar hopped to his son's branch and looked into the eyes of his past. "I'll enjoy telling Helen we found each other today."

"Yes. Give her my hellos and honks would you? Well, we're off to the shores and grasses for lunch. I'm sure we'll see you here again sometime." Stiltz hopped to an outer branch and took off toward the Gulf. Eleven ibis hidden away appeared from the depths of the tree and followed Stiltz creating a formation as they fell in behind him on the wing.

Todd looked around to see if there were any others requiring negotiations for the claiming. The tree was empty and silent.

"Well, shall we get on with it?" Todd led the moment by flying to the top of the tree and perching at one of the highest branches. And then looked down, "And we're waiting for what?"

Edgar flew off, around and perched on a top branch, looking down he grinned, "We're only waiting for him." Edgar dipped his head toward his son.

Jack called out his claiming call, flew out and around the top of the tree, the middle of the tree and then swooped up to land at the very top of the very tallest point of his tree, calling loudly. His father joined and Todd added his crow call of acknowledgment.

The pine tree next to the creek, across the way from the lake, that shaded the yellow house every morning, now belonged to Jack Crow. To share while he built his life and his crow story. And that was the bothersome question that sat in Jack's mind as his perched on his tree with his best friend and father in witness. What was his crow story and did he need this tree for it at all?

*****

The crow calls were loud and raucous. Loud enough to trigger calls from her macaws. Her macaws were far louder than the crows, outnumbered or no. Lisa walked to the window to look out at the pine tree to see who was what out there. Butters jumped on her shoulder to gaze through the glass. Snickers, her scarlet macaw flew to the other side of the window to pretend to look out, because they were looking out. But Snickers had little interest in things outside the window. Unless they were Dad. Or any moving thing, animal or human. But mostly Dad.

Snickers was born to take care of his territory. He was a scarlet macaw and he was a 'he', not a she. Boy scarlet macaws are hardwired to do perimeter checks. Butters was hardwired to hate turtles coming out of her creek across the way. She did not trust those slimy dinner plates sliding across her grasses and things. She could never prove it, but there were a number of times she could hear them hurl insults in her direction. Slimy dinner plates.

"Someone sounds like they are letting us know they are ready for lunch!" Lisa kissed Butters on the beak. "Let's get crow snacks ready. And maybe we'll find some for you guys, too!" She winked at Snickers with that last line. Maybe had nothing to do with it. It was snack time for all. And they all knew it.

She asked Butters to step up onto her cage door and walked into the kitchen sans parrot to make Jack lunch. From the sound of things, he may bring a few friends. Sometimes it felt like a double dog dare from the universe. Can she create crow pleasing meals? Can she do that while making parrot pleasing snacks? And can she do all that while making popcorn for her dozen visiting ducks? She loved a good dare. She relished a triple dog dare.

Tempting crows wasn't much different from tempting a parrot. They spoke the same language of honesty and trust building. In that, this whole game felt familiar. She liked Jack and Barbossa. They made her smile, like Edgar and Helen did so long ago. Well, maybe not so long, but two seasons for sure. Jack felt familiar. She pulled peanut butter, the flax crackers, and cashew jar out of the pantry. Parrot or crow, these items were winners. She grabbed the blueberries from the refrigerator on a whim. "Let's see how these play." She knew her macaws would appreciate them. She did not know how her crows would.

"I'm going in!" Todd jumped off his branch and soared toward the yellow house and its fence. Edgar called out and followed. Jack having no good answer to his own life questions decided one simple answer. Yes, I'm ready for lunch.

They landed on the fence in near unison. Edgar looked around. "Wow! These ducks weren't here in my time!"

A female Muscovy near the fence looked up at Edgar, "Maybe you need to get out more, crow." She tilted her head and then waddled back to foraging. Melinda had no time for thinking about crows not noticing obvious things.

Todd covered a laugh while Jack looked to see the expression on his father's face. It was exactly as he imagined it might be.

Todd looked over to the deck. "So how does this work? Do you lead the hellos Edgar, or does Jack do it now since he claimed the tree. I'm not one to step on the toes of tradition and trained humans." He was also not one to let formality impede lunch. Before Jack or Edgar could answer, Todd was already on the deck, perched on a chair. He called out.

It should be understood that claiming a house, a human, a tree or the like idea does not create any exemption of these items but rather lends to the understanding that end of day, the claim maker can, if they choose, make rules. Jack had no interest in making rules. It seemed suspicious at best to create rules for others to follow when he himself can't even decide a few simple facts about himself. Todd calling his trained human out was not without precedent nor was the action out of bounds socially. But Jack was not going to let him have first dibs of whatever she brought out.

"Shall we dad?"

"I wonder if she'll remember me at all?" Edgar asked as they both took flight to that familiar place.

They all three called to each other and to the window. Better to let her know early how many are here for dinner.

Lisa heard the calls and took a quick look through the kitchen pass through out onto the deck. Three! How lovely. She filled the paper plate in front of her with equal shares for three visitors and walked through the bird room to open the door onto the deck. Butters gave her a look of annoyance.

"Aw, baby Butterbean, no worries. You'll get yours when I'm finished serving them." Lisa stepped out onto the deck.

Butters relaxed. When mom called her Butterbean, she always brought the best treats.

"Edgar! Edgar it's you! Where have you been?" Lisa was genuinely happy and more amazed to find her favorite crow back and on her deck waiting for lunch. She knew it was Edgar by his head and neck feathers. And one wing had an always missing primary feather spot. He always looked a mess. She could pick out his disheveled profile at dusk on a powerline. She fell in love with Edgar from the very first day when he sat on a chair on the deck and dropped shells on the deck floor.

"Edgar this is wonderful. I missed you!" She set out portions for each visitor.

"This is for you, Jack." She placed his cashews, blue berry, and peanut cracker carefully in front of him.

"This is for you Barbossa." Placing same and equal in front of him.

Edgar laughed, "BARBOSSA!?"

"Leave it alone Edgar. I still got good eats!" Todd shook off the naming issue and dug in.

"By the way you two are talking I'd say we have a flock here. I'll leave you to lunch. Thanks for bringing Edgar, Jack!" And again Lisa left with a smile and kind words in her wake. Which is a very crow thing to do.

Edgar couldn't quite start eating. He was dumbfounded lady human had remembered him so easily. "Did you hear that boys? My human remembered me! You know that doesn't happen very often." Jack could see the pride clear as sunshine on his father's face.

"She's pretty sharp Dad." Jack answered, "You made an impression."

Todd spoke with his beak full, "Yeah 'nd you train'd her great, too! This is delicious!"

*****

Another thing about crows is gossip. Gossip may be too strong a word, let's call it surveillance. One quiet crow, in an orange tree not far from the yellow house, watched Jack, Todd, and Edgar eat lunch at the service of a human. It was his job to survey. He headed back to the flock trees on the other side of the neighborhood.

To a human's way of thinking this could be construed as that awful social practice of talking behind another's back. In all crow reality though it is simply a main flock, keeping an eye on the micro flocks that break off during the day. Crows don't have cell phones or GPS tracking. So every crow of a flock take turns keeping an eye on little flock break offs. Their job is returning to the main flock and report in to the family members of the crows who've wandered off. Reports aren't going to be delivered unless there is a problem, or a revelation. The only way a surveying crow can not complete their mission is if a flock member leaves their murder area. Leaving for other places not known is not the job of a surveying crow.

Today's sentinel crow, Gordon, decided what he'd just witnessed needed to be reported back to Helen and the rest of the flock. A tree claiming and lunch celebration is noteworthy. And Gordon, being Gordon, wanted to be the noteworthy presenter. He was excellent at gathering facts, keeping the facts straight and delivering the facts succinctly.

He flew out of the orange tree with a purposeful wing flap heading due south toward the three tall pine trees standing proud in the middle of a patch of saw cabbage palm near a pond. Flock Central. In the pine tree to the left of the middle of three pines, Helen perched resting out the heat of the day. No point in flying hither and thither in this heat. She never could understand how Edgar enjoyed constant dithering in the heat such as it is. She happily stayed near the flock trees, enjoyed meals with her friends and took full advantage of an empty nest. Crow retirement was just what she needed after nesting her fair share of flock families. She pondered her husband's adventurous nature and slowly became aware of her name being spoken.

Gordon landed in the middle tree. "Have you seen Helen?" He started with an elder crow, Marie. She had not, and also had not earlier.

"Excuse me, do you know where Helen is perched?" Dora did not.

"Helen, is she here?" Philip knew nothing. Of course for Philip that was the norm. Gordon hopped from the top branch down to the bottom branches inquiring of his fellow flock members. It was the hottest time of day, and all sensible crows stayed in the shade of their trees napping or preening for a later flight to forage.

He asked Jill, "Have you seen Helen?" Jill, preening her feathers for the early evening flight to come smiled and answered, "Yes I have. She's in the first tree, 9th branch on the right."

Had Gordon asked Jill about any member's whereabouts most likely she would have known, or had a good guess while not knowing. Jill was by definition a girl crow. She held to the crow code. She had plans of family and a tree and a good crow husband. She knew exactly what she was going to do as a good crow and didn't have any issue or wondering about alternatives. She is a crow, and therefore she will crow to the best of her ability.

"Thank you Jill! I should have just asked you first." Gordon grinned as he turned around.

"It would have saved you some time!" Jill said matter-of-factly. "Is everything okay for Helen? Do I need to spread word of her needing help?"

"Oh no! It is good news. Jack claimed the tree Helen and Edgar had claimed back in the day. You know, the one by the yellow house, next to the creek and a bit off from the lake." He turned around, excited to tell the news right away. And yet lingered knowing Jill and he could discuss the exciting details right now.

"That is good news! Helen will be so happy to hear." Jill thought on Jack. When they were younger, they foraged together. And once fledged they helped each other become strong flyers. But as time passed she became more crow, and he became, distracted. Her best girlfriends would comment how they were a perfect match and wouldn't it be good for Jack and Jill to become a couple. She would agree, but he would be off to disappear for a day, crow knows where. Hearing Jack had claimed his father's tree surprised her. Crows don't claim trees unless they were going to create a family and all. But then, how could that be since Jack was so very much distracted that he didn't even bother to date any crow she knew? And every crow knows you do not date outside your flock. He was always distracted, but he was never rogue.

As she lost her thoughts inside her dreamy ideas, Jerry flew in and landed hard on the branch above her. She looked up and shook her head in response. Why Jack and Todd tolerated this guy, she did not know. But for sake of flock and friends, she too would.

"Hi Jerry." She looked up and then back to Gordon.

"Gordo! Did I hear you say Jack claimed a tree? Because that is news!" Jerry looked down, head cocked to the left with crazed Jerry eyes.

"Gordon. My name is Gordon, Jerry. You know I don't appreciate your nickname of me. And yes, Jack claimed a tree. He's there now with his father and Todd." Gordon rolled his eyes and shook his head in exasperation. Jerry, it seemed, would never become a good crow.

"Well then! I better beat wings and get there. Which tree Gordo?" Jerry hopped to face the other way on his branch.

"You know the tree, his dad claimed it back in the day. It's by the yellow house north of here and stop calling me Gordo!" He'd had his fill of Jerry for today.

"Thanks Gordonski!" and with that nickname change delivered over his shoulder, Jerry disappeared heading due north.

Gordon wearing his exasperated face, looked at Jill. "I can not believe that guy is a crow."

*****

The reason Jack and Todd tolerated Jerry was the same reason they tolerated rain. It was inevitable. You can't fight a rain storm anymore than you can fight a Jerry. When the three crows were young and learning the crow ropes, Jerry was a different bird. He fit in; he didn't try not to fit in. And then that day came where he, far earlier than any other crow his age, decided he was old enough to claim a tree, and start the business of crow life.

He picked a tree next to a farm. Which made all the sense in the world for a crow. Inside the farmhouse lived a widower human. Which again made sense, his human had no distractions.

What he didn't realize was that his human, being older, had a hard time remembering training. And time. And Jerry. It's near impossible to train a forgetful human. But Jerry being young and certain of his correctness persevered through weeks of trainings.

He kept things simple. Get this old human to remember to bring apple slices when he visited. This seemed reasonable. It took one week to get his human to bring an apple slice. Jerry certain of things, paid with grass clumps and one rock. His human did not consider this a good item, but saw it as mess and dirt ending up on his porch table. And as forgetful older men tend to do, he blamed the squirrels. Which caused problems with the squirrels in the tree he had negotiated and claimed weeks earlier.

"Hey Jerry!" One squirrel, after being shooed off the porch with a broom and hearing the old man blame him for the grass and rock being laid at his feet confronted the problem head on. "How did I get to be the bad guy in your little crow family idea? HUH? I mind my business. I don't take your apple slice. I stay on my side of the tree." Jerry agreed without a word, but nodded his head. He knew he had problems now.

"HEY, Jerry!" Squirrel stood up on his hind legs flicking his tail. "You think I like being the bad guy? You think I like seeing squirrel traps sitting around for me to dodge? You think I LIKE that Jerry?" Squirrel put nose to beak on that last question.

"No. No, of course not squirrel!" He wasn't sure what answer to give but he knew a short answer would be the best.

"I suggest you straighten out the problem." Squirrel backed off Jerry's beak and stood square paw to talons.

"I suggest you straighten out the problem by finding another house and human to confuse with your offerings. I've had this guy straight for 4 years with no problems. Four years Jerry!"

Squirrel spun on one squirrel heal and stomped off to run up the tallest tree. Jerry stayed in place. This wasn't what he'd planned. You perch at night thinking things through long and hard. Making sure you've got the details covered and the human properly sorted. How many nights he lost sleep was up for debate, but certainly all this was not in the thoughts conjured on sleepless nights. He'd have to think harder. In the light. To make sure the details were clear. Jerry took three steps back and launched into flight heading to a tree off the property of the forgetful farmer and his angry squirrel.

That was the day Jerry made a decision contrary to the Crow Code. In the tallest tree not on a forgetful farmer's property Jerry vowed to focus on the Jerry Code. And he'd write that code as things happened. No point in ruling options out before the problem shows itself. He'd done that and the problem of an irritated squirrel had no answers in the Crow Code. That alone proved the crow code useless.

Seasons passed with Jerry growing certain of the genius of the Jerry Code. He didn't tell his friends about his code. No point in inviting Crow Code believers in. They'll argue points they know nothing about. None had wrestled with a forgetful farmer and irritated squirrel at the same time. They have no idea the depths of perplexity waiting an innocent crow.

Jerry flew with his Jerry Code tucked away in the back of his mind. He soared through the winds to his destination, Jack and his Crow Coded choice. The longer he soared the winds the stronger his conviction to one point. Jack had to be saved. Jack had to be saved from a dire ending.

At the very least Jack had to be saved long enough to learn his own Jack Code. And then, if after comparing the codes he still wanted the crow way, well fine. He'd done his part as a friend. It would simply be a process of introductions and a season of adventuring to the places only Jerry knew. No other crow from the flock ventured out further than the outer limits of the largest flock gatherings. Jerry had wiped out those borders seasons ago. He had a virtual second life, living side by side with where he flew at the moment. No one knew of what and who he knew.

Jerry was determined to make sure Jack knew. Because not knowing was the worst idea to Jerry. He friend Jack Crow had to know, too.

*****

Jerry came upon the creek in a quick flight's time. He followed it to the end where the yellow house sat. He didn't see a crow in the big pine tree next to the house, nor on the fence lining the yard of the house. Jerry lighted on a power line next to the creek to consider his options.

"She brings better food than when you were a fledge, Jack!" Edgar finished his last of the dinner offer. "I need to get back to your Mother. She worries."

"Bah E'gar." Todd's beak was still full.

"Okay Dad. Thanks for coming to my tree claiming. Tell mom I love her. And I love you, too." Jack smiled as big a smile as a crow could smile. His crop was full, his friend and father witnessed his negotiation of 12 ibis, and Lady Human remembered everything! What a day. It was perfect. Jack watched his dad on the wing growing smaller with the distance.

So much sky. So many options and ideas to think. Jack looked over to his good friend Todd. He sat half asleep now. Too full to fly, and with no reason to try. Jack admired Todd's way of sticking to the crow code. It all just came naturally to him. He never questioned things. Never wondered about the sky and where it could take a crow if only they kept flying. Jack's mind wandered full of thoughts. His crop full of food. There wasn't anything wrong with perfect. Except that it was perfect.

Jerry caught the sight of Edgar leaving the porch of the yellow house. He followed Edgar's trajectory and found his friends napping surrounded by leftovers.

"HEY! What are you two not doing?" Jerry flared his wings for emphasis. "Who sleeps on such a glorious afternoon begging for exploration!?"

"Jerry seriously!" Todd flapped wings and jumped to the next clear spot making a space between himself and the most annoying crow on the planet.

Before Jack could remind Jerry of his status as the most annoying crow on the planet, Lady Human appeared.

"Well, hi there crow! Jack you have another friend. How nice. What shall I call you?" Lisa looked over at Barbossa. "What do you think Barbosa, how about Twigg?" Todd laughed so hard he lifted himself off the table.

"It's decided! Twigg it is. Welcome Twigg! Eat what you like. There's still lots here." And with that Lisa walked back into the yellow house.

"Hi TWIG." Todd pronounced the name loud and clear. He lifted himself further, laughing.

"Barbossa." Jerry bowed his head low acknowledging nothing other than the food he picked up. "So boys how long you gonna stay here and be uninspired?" He swallowed the blueberry for emphasis. "And while I'm at it, how does your human get YOUR name right and ours wrong? Explain that!"

Jack startled for the question. He hadn't taken note on that truth. And why did she get his Dad's name right, too? That's the trick of life. You find an answer and then there are 10 questions from the discovery. How could everything he needs to know be here? Jack looked at Jerry and shrugged an answer to Jerry's question.

"Yeah, I thought you didn't know." He swallowed another blueberry.

"Jerry what are you doing here, anyway. You don't even like tree claiming." Todd looked over at Jerry with suspicion and a slight itch. Jerry had a tendency of tipping branches and making birds shift position. He didn't want to see Jack's position get jostled. He was already shaky as it was.

"I missed the claiming. So all's well Todd. Hey, Jack I'm taking a little expedition out into the other world. Visit friends. You wanna come?"

"I knew it! You aren't here for Jack. You're here for your own Jerry Code. You don't care about the flock. And you want to drag Jack right into the mess you call your life. Jack doesn't need your version of life Jerry. Have a nice trip. ALONE!" Todd had perched himself between Jack and Jerry.

Lisa watched the scene from her window overlooking the deck. Butters on her shoulder. "Wow, Butterbean, it looks like Barbossa has a problem with Twigg. Look at all that showboating."

Butters preened her shoulder feathers while taking a glance out the window. Jack didn't look bothered to her. And those other two crows didn't bother her. It added up to nothing to a parrot's point of view. She opted to fall asleep on her chosen shoulder. Obviously the nosey curiosity of her human would keep them there a while.

"Guys, guys let's not argue." Jack wanted this to end now. Jerry and Todd could get into big drawn out arguments that never ended in anything but questions. And hard feelings. Jerry lowered his shoulders and hopped back to a side location to Jack. Todd apologized.

"I'm sorry guys. I forget sometimes. It's not in me to think like a crow all the time. Congratulations on your tree and human Jack. This is a big deal."

Todd gave crow side eye in Jerry's direction. And relaxed his stance on the table. There was no fighting Jerry. There was no winning his mindset. "So now what? We've got the sun setting and just enough time to get on the wing home. Or are you staying in your pine tree tonight Jack?" Todd wanted to move the subject off any idea of leaving a perfect plan.

"Let's go back home. I want to thank Dad again and see what mom thinks on all this." Jack looked up into the sky's changing blue to purple.

"And Jill?" Jerry winked and nodded a knowing look at Jack.

"Slow down Jerry." Jack laughed, "I claimed the tree. That's enough for one day!"

 Music to Jerry's ears. You can claim a tree and still adventure the world.

Jerry laughed with Jack and Todd kept his gaze level at both. He didn't like Jerry and his ideas. Even when he wasn't talking about them.

*****

"The secret to happiness is the why. You can't know the why of your happiness until you know yourself. And Jack, you can't make others happy if you aren't happy with yourself." His mother's words hung in his mind still fresh from their conversation at his parent's tree. She always had a way of acknowledging his problems by explaining them. She could have just said, "Jack you're confused." But he'd be on his branch still stuck. With her maternal filter working it's magic on a son, Jack decided it was okay to be uncertain. He had his mother's understanding. He'd need it. He'd be leaving soon.

They perched looking off into a distance Jack had never trekked. Jerry's perception was further into the distance. He knew exactly who and what was out there. And he knew Jack needed to know. "Did you want to go tell everyone we're heading out into the big world?"

Jack rested his gaze as far as he could on the horizon. "No. Dad will guess and Mom knew all along. Jill will want to ask questions I can't answer. Let's go." With a tilt forward Jack slipped off the branch and into the winds. A trust fall to the universe. Jerry fell in and beside Jack as they swooped up and into the higher jet stream.

"Trust me Jack. We'll be back and you'll know. And then you can know your why. I found mine out there."

The wind carried them to a point only Jerry knew. The sights and sounds were familiar. Jack had thought adventuring would take him to places strange and queer. "Where are we headed Jerry?"

"See that water?"

Jack looked on the horizon to see a body of water growing quickly. How had so much water been right here all along? No one had mentioned this water. Not one crow, ever. They hadn't been in the air long enough for something so... unexpected. This was too close to be amazing and new.

"I don't understand Jerry? We aren't that far from home. How can all this be so close!"

"Jack, you don't have to go far to find out what you don't know. Wait until you meet Ardon. He knows more than any other bird I have ever met! And I've met quite a few. I want you to meet them all."

With that wish Jerry dove toward a forest of trees on the edge of a bay. Jack fell in line and trajectory. Jerry's confidence where they were about to land seemed certain. Until the egret. Egrets by nature pay little attention to other birds. Standing four feet tall with a wingspan twice that makes a bird certain he's not in need of any other bird's permission. Ardon lighted on the exact mangrove branch Jerry had targeted. Jerry expected that, veered left and chose the neighboring mangrove tree, it's branch longer and more accommodating for two.

Jack took in the salt air brought in by the winds he descended from. He landed on the branch next to Jerry and looked to the egret on the next tree.

Egrets were nothing new to Jack, he'd just never had the opportunity to speak to one. They seemed far to busy for idle chit chat. Jerry settled his feathers flat and heaved a sigh. Ardon did same and heaved a fish down his throat. Jack waited to see what came next.

"Ardon! Meet Jack. He's a friend of mine. We're on an adventure to find Jack's why."

"Finding a why is an important step in finding your how. You can't find the how without the why." It seemed egrets here were just as disinterested in idle chit-chat. Jack pondered Ardon's words, not knowing what his other options were for the moment.

"Exactly what I told you last week, Jack!"

The three sat silent on neighboring mangrove trees. Jack felt as though he should say something. The silence was thick as fog. Jerry seemed content to look out into the water and think. Or whatever it was Jerry did when he wasn't talking. He looked in Jerry's viewing direction to watch the water move. The sound of the water washing against the shore near their trees and the view of moving water coupled with swaying branches in winds. Jack felt sleep arrive.

"Jack look there!"

Jack woke fast out of a hard nap to look past the point of Jerry's beak.

"See that! That's a dolphin. I met one once. They laugh and play all day. It's impossible not to enjoy a dolphin's company." Jerry's grin convinced Jack of his opinion.

Ardon stirred. "Dolphin breath air. If you are near a dolphin when they breech the surface of the water to take a breath, you will hear life's struggle rewarded with more life."

Jerry's eyes grew enormous, he slowly nodded toward Ardon and grinned, thumbing a pointed wing feather toward his mentor. "I have no idea what he said Jack, but I'm smarter for hearing it."

Silence resumed. Jerry perched to nap with his knees now bent, moving body weight forward to relax. Ardon had yet to move a muscle or feather since landing and swallowing his fish. It seemed he knew where to put himself naturally. Jack wondered how that must feel, just knowing.

The sun moved over the water slowly changing the glints and glares of the waves. A nap felt appropriate. Jack closed his eyes, but kept a good grip on the tree branch. Jerry could wake him again for another surprise. He would be ready.

*****

"Jill have you seen Jack?" Todd perched across the tree branch waiting for an answer. Jill looked up from her nestled nap slightly befuddled. These three crows needed her to find each other more and more these days. She shook her head no. Why fully waking up from a good nap to say no?

"Well, do you have a guess?" Todd looked past her indignation to a point on the other side of the tree.

"A guess? Why would I bother guessing anything about Jack Crow. I guess he's more interested in doing what he wants than what the flock needs! How's that for a guess?"

Todd knew when to quit, and that when was now. "Okay. Gotcha. Why would you guess about any of this Jack's location business. He's just missing. Jerry's missing, too. Unrelated misplaced crows ..." He paused for affect.

"Wait. Jerry and Jack are missing? I've got another guess for you. I guess we'll know where they are when they get back from Jerry's idea of acting the crow. You may as well finish your nap here." Jill worked her beak back into her shoulder feathers to close her eyes.

Crows. Boy crows. Lost little chicks wondering the woods. She couldn't remember when she told any of them she'd be their mother.

Todd stared across the tree branch at Jill. Finish taking a nap here? What did she mean by that, was this a first date, or did she want him to shut up? Or maybe Jack was not missing at all. He and Jerry were around here laughing under their wings waiting to jump on his branch and make a joke at his expense. Todd didn't move. This is just the laugh Jerry prized. Jill's breathing slowed to a quiet rhythm. If this was a setup, her involvement was slim. Her nap was sincere.

She had a point. If Jerry and Jack were off to places only Jerry knew, their absence could be awhile. He relaxed his feet. The breeze moved his branch lulling his eyes. The air was cool, the sun warm, his shaded spot perfect. No need to stay awake only to wait on things to unfold.

At the edge of a bay, and the center of a flock's forest, separate crows napped the night through. Crow, or any bird worth their weight, do not sleep all the night through. They nap. They nap, wake, resettle, see who else is awake, and nod goodnap to each other.

Egrets do the same, but with less waking and more napping. The morning comes quicker that way. Jack and Jerry had exercised true crow night napping checking with each other ever so breezy often. The morning came slower to their side of the mangrove tree.

*****

Jill woke first light and sought out Edgar and Helen right off. She napped less than usual last night considering the irritant of rogue crow possibilities. It was always left to the girls to get the boys in line. Her mother warned her long ago of this flocking requirement. "Jill, don't be fooled for a second when all the boys gather to state opinions on matters they have no intention on proving. Crowing is what they do. Best to know the crowing only changes when the right girl sets her mind to it."

She set her mind to letting Jack's parents know about their son and Jerry off gallivanting crow knows where. She found Edgar on the ground foraging not far from Helen who perched at the top of a tree. She chose to talk to Helen first lighting just below her on a bare branch. "Good Morning Helen!"

"Jill, good morning to you. What brings you here so early?"

"I found out last night Jack and Jerry are missing. Probably not missing, more likely following the whims of Jerry and his idea of living a crow life. I thought you should know straight away."

Helen paused working her wing feathers. A sigh escaped her heart and a breath left her chest. "I see. I do appreciate the information and the worry over them. Jack and Jerry. That's quite a pair. I hope the universe can stand up to them." Helen looked at Jill with a smile of confidence. No need in getting the girl more riled up.

"Well then, if this isn't a problem for you, I'll see you at breakfast tree." Smiling their goodbyes Jill left bewildered.

Helen didn't care her son was out cavorting with Jerry? How could that be? Helen was the best example of crow code following she knew! And hearing her son was following no code or worse, Jerry Code, Helen just smiled and worried for the universe? None of this made sense, and yet all of it did to some point. She didn't inform Edgar of all this because knowing Jack's father, he'd laugh and ask her to point where she last saw him fly. And fall into the trajectory hoping to find them both. Before Helen, Edgar was notorious as a thither and yon crow.

Gordon came to mind at that last thought. She'd better find him and get him up to date on things. Otherwise that crow would spend three days and 6 trees telling anyone who would sit still long enough. If Jack's parents weren't unsettled. There was little point to unsettling every one else. There were times Crow Code created unwanted results. Gordon was one of them.

At the moment Jill finished filling in Gordon on the current situation of Jack and Jerry, Ardon woke to the buzzing sounds of mosquitos starting their day of blood harvesting. He shook his head and stretched his wings wide. Folded smooth once again, Ardon focused his eyes on the horizon of water and sky. The clouds gathered slowly and separated slower. Today would be a warm humid day.

The mosquitos would appreciate that forecast.

Jerry woke next. He stretched and folded his wings enjoying the feel of the warm salty air on his feathers. He looked over to Ardon to see how busy they would be today. From the looks of his mentor, not very. Jack woke only opening his eyes. There was a sense he was waking from a dream and would find himself in his home tree, not here on the edge of the water in the dream feeling moment. One eye opened allowing the second to follow with less suspicion. It wasn't a dream. He saw Jerry and Ardon laughing about that which they both found entertaining. He closed his eyes. All this seemed like a good idea yesterday. This morning, fresh eyed, he felt and saw the reality of his new world. He knew nothing. He knew less now than he did yesterday. A mosquito added a punctuation point to his thoughts by buzzing his ear. It agreed that Jack knew nothing at all.

"Morning Slumberjack!" Jerry, still laughing, greeted Jack as always. No need to change tradition just because the scenery changed.

"Greetings new friend." Ardon lowered his head and raised it to continue seeking knowledge from the sun resting on the horizon.

"Good morning. I have to say waking up on the water's edge is nice."

"Yes, the view and the inhabitants invite us to think on ourselves before we think on our day. Which is always a better way to start."

Jerry nodded and grinned toward Jack, eyes wide with a mad joy. Jerry perched leaning just slightly forward in an anticipation of hearing all things strange and above his own spectrum.

It was good to be with birds certain of things, or certain of knowing they need to know things. The fog of sleep slipped away leaving Jack ready to eat a good meal.

"Where you having breakfast Ardon?"

"I believe I'll wait longer in time to think on that need. Most likely breakfast will present itself at my feet." Jerry grinned wider. Jack nodded acknowledging the sage in their midst.

"Well, I'll take Jack for a tour of the neighborhood and neighbors, grab a bite over at the mangrove where all the boats come and go. Jack you can't believe what there is to eat until you wait for fishermen to come back from wherever they go."

Jerry burst from the mangrove branch into the winds, Jack followed. They had a dry tail wind from the land blowing out into the bay. Winds change quickly giving a visiting crow a quicker lesson. It's best to pay attention to where you're going and not where you've been.

There's a truth to water's edge living not known until you visit there. It's easier to fly. Maybe it's the winds, maybe it's the humidity, maybe it's because you can just follow the shore navigating in space not claimed by humans. It seems mangroves keep humans at bay. Whatever the reason flying this morning was an invigorating exercise in travel. Nothing was the same.

Waters lapped against sands and rock washing up turtle grasses and dead undergrowth from the bay itself. The higher they flew the more Jack could place himself inside the space. The water had an end on the other side of itself. There too, he imagined the morning unfolding as it was for him now on this side.

He kept Jerry in his vision while keeping a distance. He had no interest in conversation. Jack felt a need to take in all that he didn't know. Certainly he knew less now than he did yesterday. Was this life? With every exploration you find new things you don't know? Could any crow be certain of anything, let alone the Crow Code?

They dove a hundred feet lower to skim trees as they left the mangrove lining the shore. "Jack! Look there!"

Jack gazed toward Jerry's flight to see these things he referred to as boats. Boats seemed like cars. They carried humans. They were noisy. And there were a lot in an area that seemed too small to accommodate them. The mangroves thinned here, opening to clear water with paths built for the humans and their boats to stop. These must be the fishermen. There were a few fishermen lined up at a table on the docks where they tied their boats. There they cut fish to pieces and shapes. Jerry laughed and shouted, "Breakfast is served!" He nose-dived to perch next to one of the fisherman. The real question now was, did Jerry have that guy trained?

Jack perched further down the rail to the left of Jerry who was to the left of this fisherman. Gull screamed and called hovering in the air directly in front of the fisherman. He acknowledged none of them, but tossed fish heads and bones into the air haphazardly in their direction. This resulted in an explosion of arguments between the gulls who owned that piece of haphazard breakfast. Jerry cawed into the wind laughing like a mad crow. Jack waited to see if someone trained this guy.

"Do you know this human, Jerry?"

"No. There's always a different guy."

"Well, how can any of this work? You need the same human every day to train."

"Jack relax. Crow Code doesn't work out here. Just wait. I kid you not it works without all that code business!"

If that guy wasn't trained he sure acted like it at that moment. With no work at all on Jerry's part, he plopped a wad of fish skin next to Jerry's feet without saying a word or being paid. Jerry swallowed it and flapped his wings. Jerry looked at Jack with an oily grin. And winked.

Jack said not a word as the guy then laid fish guts at his own feet without a glance. That was one whole meal with absolutely no work involved. The guy didn't even know him! The gulls called out consternation. They'd waited two rounds and had enough of crow being fed first.

"I'd eat that now Jack, you can't beat a gull over breakfast."

Jack swallowed greedily. Can't beat a gull over breakfast. Good to know.

Ill-content gull filled the air around and above Jack and Jerry. The fishermen continued their fish cleaning, keeping most but sharing some, with any bird that presented an open mouth. Jack perched in disbelief. Boats came and left each with it's own flurry of gulls following. This was an open secret! Yet not known by any crow he knew! A full crop kept him perched. He had little interest in flying, nor did Jerry. They turned around in their perched position to once again look out onto the waters and mangroves. The winds were calming; the day was settling into itself. With no effort on Jack's part he too, settled into himself. That sensation was new.

Jerry sidestepped to Jack's side. "Hey, we should go visit the twins. They are hilarious!"

"Twins? Human or crow?"

"Jack do you have to know everything before you learn anything?" Jerry jumped into the winds opening his wings to harness their powers.

Jack followed in kind. They left the gulls, boats, and their fishermen behind as they gained altitude and headed toward a large patch of grass and flowers between houses. Three old oaks, heavy limbed, stood tall in a row at the edge. Jack saw full bird feeders and blue jay surrounding them in the grass. This all seemed more familiar, except for the bright pink birds with spoons for bills. He made a mental note to know more about them.

Jerry landed at the top of the middle oak and settled his wings. Jack joined him on a lower branch. Jerry laughed and dropped himself into the air below to coast into a winged landing next to a blue jay not surprised by his arrival.

Jack looked down, Jerry and twin blue jays looked up. Before he could drop to the green floor a voice behind him sounded. "Psst! Jack is that you?"

Jack turned to look behind and below to see a pair of eyes peering out of the dense green leaves of the oak. There was something in those eyes that reminded him of someone at home. But who? "Yes it's me, Jack. Who are you?"

Stiltz burst through the leaves scrambling the branch toward Jack. "So here you are and there you aren't! Jerry must be here then."

"How do you know about...wait a minute. What are YOU doing here Stiltz?"

"I'm here every other day. You need to get out with other than crow to know these things Jack."

"Yes I'm learning that today."

"I just wanted to say hello. My flock are waiting in that tree over there by the beach. It's time to eat sand fleas."

"Sand fleas?" The words left his beak confused as they felt, but Stiltz had already gained lift and loft toward his flock's location. Jack turned his attention to Jerry and his twins. Jerry had joined them at the bird feeder hanging from a pole. He hoped there were no sand fleas in that, and realized if there were he'd have no idea.

Knowing around here came fast. Too fast. So many questions born from things now known. Jack looked up again to the ibis flock foraging in the sands for their fleas. He'd leave that unknown detail for later consideration. He looked past them further into the sun to the waters beyond waves turned white at the edges crashing into themselves. Gull, osprey and cormorant traveled the winds. These were knowns. They visited the lake across from his yellow house. He could easily watch them from the top of his tree.

Boats filled with humans traveled to and from the spots they would stop. Sometimes they formed lines like ants all heading in the same direction. Sometimes they looked like floating mosquitos in all directions with no particular place to go and trying to get there quickly.

The winds were changing again, bringing the salty air to the land. That was a smell he liked. Jack was becoming aware that the more questions came from the more he knew, the more he knew what he liked and did not. This was a new sensation. Salty winds ruffled his shoulder feathers. He closed his eyes, pointed his beak into the winds and let his mind wonder through his new sensations and truths.

The best thing about being a crow is being your own crow. Jack was certain of this new truth. I am my own crow. Self affirmation circling his thoughts. Jack also felt certain that his own flock back home were not their own crows. Uncertain as they were about doing uncertain things. Jack's wandering memory conjured a day long ago when he flew down to a fence to see about a commotion. His flock stayed perched in the family tree while he dove headfirst into the fray. They stayed in the tree yelling warnings down.

"Come back!"

"You'll die!"

"Don't sit there!"

Nothing happened. Nothing happened because nothing generally happens. His parents told stories about humans and the little ones throwing rocks at crows on fences. Jack decided after the day he inspected the commotion of a non commotion that until someone threw a rock at him he'd better investigate things. What's the point of being able to fly if you're afraid to fly? You can't just not fly. Even before Jack had all these new answers, that opinion seemed quite crow. Today as he inhaled sea salty mists and listened to the gulls cavil he added one more truth to himself. You can't listen to stories and believe them just because someone tells them. You fly to your own truths.

The winds were arguing among themselves. Jack felt their disagreement. Some came from the North rushing over his feathers and past his ears with a whoosh. Others surprised his relaxed wings with pressures from the East. Jack held his wings closer to his body for the wind's strength. He breathed deep and slow allowing the air carrying smells and sounds to wash over him. A slight shake of his branch pulled him back from his breathing. He didn't open his eyes, he'd rather not if he could avoid it. The rustle to his right and left forced him to peek.

The twins once on the ground with Jerry were now perched on both his sides, they carried welcoming smiles and an unhinged look in their eyes. Jack opened his eyes knowing he wouldn't be alone for the rest of the afternoon.

Blue jays do not accept no for an answer. They also rarely ask questions to give you that opportunity. A blue jay is a blue dart with a loud voice and strong opinion. One tends to stay out of their way, if one is smart.

"Hi Jack!" They spoke in a chorus with one voice leading ever so slightly the other. As if one twin was trailing the thought of the other by one word. It was almost a song, and thoroughly off putting. He rustled his feathers to pull his mind back in sync with his body. This conversation would require his full attention. He looked to his right and left taking in the sight of twin blue jays. Identical in voice and feather.

"Hello." Jack kept it short without inquiry. A proven strategy when dealing with blue jays, identical or not.

"My name is Petra!" She perched high on her taloned toes to his right.

"I'm Seta!"

Jack looked to his left at her introduction, and then right again nodding he'd heard them clearly. "Nice to meet you both."

"Yes! It is!" Their chorused sing song response rang out into the northern winds. "Are you staying up here all day to sleep or are you going to come down and eat?"

Jack looked down toward the ground to find Jerry looking up laughing. Jerry's collection of interesting friends proved he had no interest in staying in his murder to live out a life of isolated experiences. Once you meet an identical set of blue jays who speak at the same time while saying the same thing without failure, an ibis in a pine tree becomes inadequate.

Jack used the arguing winds to spiral his way down to Jerry's grassy area. The Twins didn't bother to spiral, nor did they bother to stop talking.

"Girls! Thanks for getting a crow out of a tree!"

"You're welcome Jerry. Your friend thinks too much, we can tell."

Jack stood in belly high grass looking at the twins, with a mild case of amusement. No point in taking blue jays serious. They barely do that with themselves. The girls hopped in place trying to stay above the tall grass. The winds picked them up and set them down gently.

"I've got an idea Jack!"

"I wake up assuming you do Jerry."

"We are going to eat our fill with the girls this morning, and then go to the amusement park!"

Jack began to form the words, what's an amusement park, and thought better of it. He didn't need to know at this point. And knowing would most likely bring more questions. Petra and Seta seemed excited about the prospect though.

"OH!" their voices chimed in unison. "We were there all day yesterday! Such a lovely day. We found a little girl eating little girl popcorn and she found us. Her popcorn was delicious! You should find her while you are there!" Petra caught a gust of northern wind at the same time Seta rode an easterly breeze. They seemed frozen in time, floating on winds together.

"Ladies I'm doing one better than a girl with popcorn. I'm going to introduce Jack here, to Conrad!"

"Oooooo! Really? How very exciting for you both!"

Jack watched the girls sink again into the tall grass, with looks of surprise and admiration. They were impressed by his future.

"Jack doesn't know a giraffe from a rock. I'm looking forward to seeing him meet his first giraffe."

Petra looked Jack in the eye, leaning through the tall grass. She tilted her head and leaned just a little closer to whisper her secret. "If you don't know a giraffe isn't a rock, you should know giraffes are geniuses. All of them. Don't ask silly questions, only good ones." She leaned back, tip toe upright smiling in satisfaction. It was obvious she felt her ideas were priceless and informative.

Giraffes are genius. It's true. If you've not met a giraffe you may not know this fundamental natural idea. All giraffes are genius. Those that know a giraffe or have had the chance to seek counsel from a giraffe know this truth to be self evident.

There's an upside to living in a zoo. If it's a good zoo. The zoo Jerry and Jack took to the winds to visit was contained inside an amusement park. This is neither good, or bad. Generally for visiting birds it's good because the humans that visit the park eat and leave messes. A feast any crow would fly to enjoy.

"The upside for the residents of a zoo in an amusement park is there are no problems. Living in the wild is nothing but problems. Wake up, is there food? Look around. Am I food? Every day is nothing but problems. You worry about being eaten and finding something to eat at the same time. I don't know about you Jack, but I've seen others crack under the pressure."

Jack followed Jerry on the Eastern winds heading over the waters. Jerry's excitement cut through the air. Once Jerry was onto an opinion there was no stopping him. Jack listened while his eyes wandered the waterscape speeding past them. Looking up he saw buildings fast approaching. Jerry took a hard left toward land. Jack followed. The horizon brought shapes and buildings Jack had never seen. He also heard screams. At first Jack thought the pitch to be gulls dictating their sarcasm to the sun. The closer the land and objects became the clearer the truth. There were humans yelling, screaming, and laughing. And they were sitting in cars with no tops that rode on tubes that tossed and turned.

He saw them screaming at the top, yelling at the bottom, and what's more, voluntarily getting into those cars at the beginning. No wonder humans didn't seem very smart. They didn't act it.

*****

Jack and Jerry descended into the winds and landed on a fence. Looking to one side of the fence Jack saw enclosures filled with all kinds of animals in all kinds of ways. Some were familiar to him, some were simply baffling to look upon. When he turned around on the fence he saw the screaming, yelling and volunteering riders just a wing away. No matter where he looked he saw humans. Walking, talking, eating, laughing or gazing. Some looked confused. Some looked tired. Most looked like they were not where they wanted to be, and were working hard to get somewhere else.

Jerry took a deep breath, filling his chest full of all the smells this place offered. "Jack, let's find Carl!"

"Is Carl the genius giraffe?"

"No, that's Conrad."

"Oh."

And with that Jerry shot himself back into the Eastern and Northern winds, choosing to let the Northern breezes take him to their next perching spot. Jack flew into the same stream following Jerry to find Carl who would eventually somehow find a genius giraffe named Conrad. Or not. At this point Jack had accepted the fact that Jerry had ideas and friends. And he mixed them up into a grab bag so as not to have too much of a plan about any of it.

"Follow me, he should be out and done with all that mingling business."

"Mingling what?"

Jerry became a black shadow in the sky before Jack could consider what mingling meant to a Carl. They flew further into the zoo side and over enclosures. Horses with stripes. Jack made a note to discuss these horses with Jerry after they found Carl. They flew. Huge grey beasts with huge grey ears and a nose that reached the ground appeared as they rounded a group of pine trees. Trees much taller than his own back home. Jack tucked this site next to the striped horses. Cats! Huge yellow cats napping in the sunshine.

Jack knew cats, at night he could hear them pouring threats into the air. High pitched and grating throat calls. They were never this huge, or this lazy. Jerry added height to their flight pattern heading into the blue sky and softening winds. They were coming from the West now. Softer. The heat of the day was slowing everything down, including the giant cats. "Jerry! The cats! How do they grow that big here?"

The Western breeze swallowed his question whole. Jerry turned into the breezes and headed straight for a line of oak trees filled with Spanish moss. The moss draped long and low brushing the ground, hiding what was behind. Jerry landed in the second from the left tree and Jack followed landing one branch above him.

Jerry opened his beak to start another tirade of thoughts and opinions but Jack cut him off. "Wait. I have questions. What were the striped horses?"

"Zebra. They aren't from around here."

"What were those huge grey flat footed long nosed guys?"

"Pachyderms. Some call them elephants. I know they call each other, Don, Sandra, Stan, and Daren and the little one is Sandra's kid, Tony."

"And the cats, how are they so big?"

"Those are lions, which are cats you don't keep in a house I guess. They aren't from around here either. I don't know why they are so big, but I know you don't have a conversation with them until after they have lunch. Jack you are hilarious. Everything's a thing with you."

"Lions are a thing, Jerry. So, where are we now?" Jack found himself perched in a tree bordering two different enclosures. He looked over his back to see wandering flamingos. He'd seen one alone near his creek once. Flamingos are a thing, but not "a thing" like a lion. He looked forward into the other enclosure to see nothing but tall grasses, taller thin trees and boulders far too ordered to be natural or real. "So this is the zoo inside the amusement part that has humans lining up so they can scream like they didn't want to be wherever they put themselves, huh?"

"Yes, it is. And this is where you find genius and snacks."

"I'm not sure about this zoo idea. Where do they find pachyderms and giant cats? And the horses with stripes, the zebras. Where'd they get those and do any of them want to be here?"

Jerry ignored the questions bombarding him. No point in answering questions that don't need answers right now. A zebra's opinion has nothing to do with snacks or genius. All of which provide a lovely afternoon if you relax. Jerry wasn't certain Jack would ever get the relax part under control. A voice from behind offered an answer to Jack's collection of inquiries.

"Zoo life is A-Okay with me."

A flamingo sauntered his way toward Jack and Jerry. He nodded acknowledgment to Jerry and continued sauntering. "I know where the food is and I know where the lions are sleeping. I know the crocodiles are in a lake with a fence. I don't mind my fence. Why should I? That fence says, "Hey. I'm here to keep the problems out there. Relax. Pull a leg up. I like my fence. I like my fence and I like my friends in here. Good friends, a fence, timely food, no lions. A flamingo can bury their beak in their feathers knowing problems can't jump a fence."

"Pardon me. I didn't mean to offend in any way. I'm just curious as to it all. I've never seen a zoo, or met a zoo resident before."

Carl lowered his head to inspect the grasses under his feet and raised it back to look at Jack. "Yes, I know. Jerry warned me he'd bring you one day. Welcome. For the record we like our flamingo perfect place. Gunter and I enjoy wondering where we please, sometimes I lead, sometime he leads. He leads in the same circle shape every day. I prefer meandering through the pond, past the plants and butterflies taking a left at the palm trees, circling back, and walking behind the rocks. Which is hilarious because that move leaves the humans standing on the other side of my fence gawking. They can't see us, so they wait. They wait looking at each other and then the rocks saying things like, "Where'd they go?" The look on their faces is priceless.

Once we stayed behind the rocks till lunch just to see what they'd do. Gunter would stick his head up above the rocks random like and we'd laugh and laugh watching the humans jump and shout, "There they are!" Humans. So easily entertained. Jerry tells me your humans are easily entertained and sometimes easily trained."

"I'm not sure about the trained part. I'm training a human myself right now. There are easy days and then there are days I'm certain I should give up. They aren't that smart."

Gunter strode into their conversation without pause or introductions. He had a bigger concern than crows. "Carl, what's mingling?"

"Mingling? I'm not sure, where d'you hear that word?"

"The Zoo folk, they were talking about mingling and flamingos. I know we're the flamingos, but I don't know what a mingling is and what that has to do with us."

The downside of zoos are zoo folk. They do a spectacular job at serving needs but then they think about things. The last time a conversation of human ideas popped up Santa's Zoo Night happened. Three weeks of zoo folk wearing Santa hats and walking around saying 'hohoho' while serving zoo residents. How a Santa's Zoo Night lasted three weeks is still unknown. Flamingos have no problem understanding time. Humans do.

Mingling. Carl knew just who to ask about this impending idea. Conrad. "Well let's go find Conrad and ask. He'll know. Jack. Jerry. You're welcome to join us if you like."

Jerry hopped into the air stream hovering a moment, yes was a word he preferred to pronounce with action.

"How far is this Conrad fellow?" Jack preferred pronouncing action with caution.

Jerry, Carl, and Gunter headed to the back corner of the Flamingo's side. Jerry landed in the shorter grasses and hopped his way next to Carl and Gunter. They didn't bother answering Jack.

Jack didn't bother to argue the point. He hopped onto the Flamingo side, onto the grassy earth and continued hopping his way near his fellow travelers. They found themselves behind boulders in cool shade. The two meeting corners of the enclosures weren't closed off. There was plenty of room for flamingos to walk behind the rocks to enter the other area. Jack and Jerry hopped behind their pink friends and found themselves in a wholly new area and environment.

Carl spoke to no one in particular. "To look at him you wouldn't know Conrad was a genius. He is, and he's 12 feet of genius packed inside a giraffe. In the wild most giraffe are geniuses. It's something few humans realize. When you are looking upon a giraffe, you are looking upon a genius."

Jack didn't say a word in answer or question. Jerry held his tongue in surprise. Jack not asking questions was as unusual as the winds not moving.

"Conrad! Hey Conrad!" He was walking looking up at the sky not too far away. "I better catch his attention. Waiting may not be a good idea considering this mingling issue." Carl walked out from behind the boulders and began an impressive attention getting dance of wing feathers and strutting. He caught Conrad's attention, and a group of humans with cameras. None of this needed any of that, he fast walked back behind the boulders. Flamingos only had two speeds on legs. Walk, fast walk. If a flamingo wanted more than that he'd have to fly.

"Carl. Good morning. Why all the shouting?"

Jack saw a spotted head reveal itself through the hanging branches. Soft brown eyes haloed in eyelashes looked on all concerned behind the boulders. Conrad had horns, but they were soft and fuzzy. And then all of Conrad settled behind the boulders shielding him from the view of gawking humans, but exposing every inch of genius giraffe to Jack and his friends.

Tall didn't begin to describe a giraffe. Tall described a tree. Towering would be a good word for Conrad. Jack looked up lifting his head a bit further for each new piece of giraffe information. Conrad's neck was longer than Conrad's legs. All of Conrad was spotted in browns, against yellows. His nose was soft his tongue long enough to swat flies from his very own eyes! Jack stared in awe at a genius giraffe. Jack's thoughts spilled off into Carl's conversation.

"Conrad I think we have a problem. Mingling. Have you heard of it and what does that mean?"

"Mingling means to visit or spend time with others. We don't have a problem though. You do. They are putting together a mingling party for the flamingos. Flamingling they are calling it. Word mash. Humans love word mash. No wonder they have a hard time understanding each other. Yesterday I listened to two zoo folk discuss having lunch and when to do it. They jabbered on for 30 minutes about eating. They make lunch as complicated as their word mash." Conrad looked down, Jack looked up. Carl looked worried.

"Flamingling?" The implications were enormous.

"Yes, Carl. Flamingling. I'd venture a guess you will spend time with random humans so they can see you up close and personal. I would doubt they will feed you. I would also doubt they will touch you. So. There's that."

Conrad strolled away. "I wouldn't worry about it. What's a little mingling among flamingos?"

Jack's gaze followed his new site. Conrad paused and looked back over to Jack. "You worry far too much crow. Today is halfway over and you're still sitting in 10 minutes ago."

Carl and Gunter were already headed back to their side, in active conversation about their future mingling. Jerry hopped over to Jack smiling. "You see that Jerry? You see that? I've learned something in my travels, the less a creature talks, the more they know. Conrad is a genius. He only says what needs saying and not a word more! Imagine the time he saves for other things."

Jerry watched the last of Conrad round the boulders heading back out into the sun and gawking gaze of humans. Jack looked over Jerry's shoulder witnessing the same Conrad exit. So many questions. At this very moment he didn't care to learn one answer.

The breezes skating over the tall grass moved him to look to the sky. He saw the dancing gull silhouettes hundreds of feet above. He was aware of being happily settled in a place and time he was unfamiliar. This was a new sensation. Jerry lighted above him back in the tree. His beak nestled into his wing. He was correct, a nap before lunch was appropriate. Jack chose to stay in the grass feeling the sway of it against his legs. He watched the flamingos walk to their water pool. They settled one leg up, no doubt still uncertain of the whole mingling idea. He didn't feel tired, he didn't feel worried. What was this state? Invigorated? Inspired? Content? Whatever it was Jack rested easy in the grass at the edge of the shade provided by a tree shorter than a genius giraffe.

He tried recalling all the trees he perched in at home, and divided them into two groups. Shorter than a genius giraffe and taller than. He'd never thought of his trees as any other idea than a tree. How fun to consider a new idea against the familiar idea!

"Pssst! Hey, you. Crow!"

Jack's wandering thoughts collected themselves so he could concentrate on locating the voice calling.

"Over here Crow!

"Jack. My name's Jack."

"Okay, Crow." At the edge of the pond, peering from long grasses and pond greenery, a turtle's head appeared. This was a big turtle. Bigger than the turtles Jack knew back home. "So, did you get anything you want to share?"

"Excuse me? Get anything? I haven't tried to get anything. Is that how it works around here? I get things and share?"

"No need to get all tense bud. I'm just asking. Your friend over there always brings me things after he's found the good leftovers. I just figured you might be like him."

The turtle left the dense grasses and walked closer to Jack. He was a big turtle with a big head, bigger brown eyes and an impressive shell. His shell had all the colors of a pond in a pattern of many circles inside circles. If he didn't want to be seen or found, Jack was certain his domed shell would make that happen.

"We've not gone looking for things as of yet, we were busy talking to Conrad about Carl and Gunter's problem."

"HA! Carla and Gunter always have a problem. Those two are always worked up about something. Which is hilarious. The way they don't act worked up you'd think they were, you know, stable. But flamingos aren't stable, their brains can't shut down. Or, something like that."

"I see, well that's good information to know. I'm new around here so all this is rather… new."

"Yeah, you look like a rogue. Jerry used to look like a rogue. Back in the day. So are you two going to go looking for stuff or what?"

"He's napping over there, so I guess we'll most likely when he wakes up. You know Jerry, his first thought is food, his last thought is sleep. He keeps it simple."

"I like that about that guy. Hey, you see the zebra?"

"Yes! Striped horses are impressive."

"I used to live over there in their waterhole."

"Oh?"

"The problem with zebra is they don't listen."

"To who?"

"What?"

"You said they don't listen. They don't listen to who?"

"OH! You're one of those guys. I see. Look what's your name again?"

"Jack."

"Jack. Okay Jack. I'm gonna go back and scrape moss off rocks. Tell Jerry I hope he brings me that burrito thing again. That was tasty."

"Wait! What's your name? And who don't the zebras listen to?" Jack watched the turtle walk back into the grasses and disappear with a splash and rustling fronds. Turtle didn't bother to answer Jack. Zebras don't listen. Jack flew to the tree and decided napping wasn't in his best interest. He had a bit of time until Jerry woke. Zebras don't listen to who? He wanted to find out.

His flight carried him over the lions. Now napping in the shade they looked like the cats at home. Stretched out and breathing slowly at rest. He hadn't noted before, but now with a second look he took in just how big their paws were. One lion lay on it's back legs stretched, paws up. The claws on those paws suggested all kinds of bad endings for any one that got in the way. He looked up continuing toward his striped horses. They too were resting, but not asleep, under a group of trees for shade. He landed in the tree nearest the zebra grazing.

"Excuse me." "Excuse me zebra." Zebra didn't react to his words and continued tugging at the grasses at his hooves. Eating methodically. "Excuse me z ..."

"Zed."

"Zed?"

"Zed. My name is Zed."

"I'm Jack!"

"Fine. Fine. What am I excusing Jack?"

"Oh. Well, I was talking to a turtle over there where the flamingos are, and I had a question."

Zed stopped eating and raised his head up to view the Crow dumb enough to talk to Terrance. "Come down and stand on the ground for me. You're too high and my neck doesn't work that way."

Jack lofted off the branch gently landed on the ground a few feet in front of Zed. Jack noticed how short the grass was here. It barely covered his feet, didn't sway in the wind or tickle his tail feathers. Zed looked down, shook his black mane of hair and picked up where his grass eating left off. "So, what did Terrance have to say that you needed to come here and clarify?"

"Terrance. That's his name. You know he wouldn't even tell me that, he just said the thing about zebras is they don't listen. And he wouldn't tell me who you don't listen to …"

Zed stopped chewing, swallowed and took two steps closer to Jack. He lowered his head so that their eyes were on equal level. He looked serious, for a striped horse named Zed.

"Do you like stories Jack?"

"Well, yes. Yes I believe I do like a good story."

"The answer to your question requires a story. A story about a turtle who hasn't learned how to ask the right questions. Do you want to hear that story Jack?" Zed cocked his head a bit, his mane hung stiff off the top of his neck.

Serious zebras look slightly annoyed now that he thought about it. Jack straightened his posture to give a serious listener attitude in response. "Yes I would like to hear that story Zed."

"Alright then. Back before the roller coasters appeared there was a lake with trees and a sloping hill."

"What's a roller coaster?"

"The train …with screaming humans getting on and off for no apparent reason."

"OH! Wait. So that wasn't there and they put it there knowing it would make other humans scream?"

"I'm not going to attempt to explain humans. That's impossible. Do you want to here a story answering your specific question, or not?"

"Yes. Yes and sorry for interrupting."

"Back before the roller coasters appeared there was a lake with trees and a sloping hill. And before that, zebras were over there, not here. Terrance was over there, too. In fact there were more turtles over there, who ended up in ponds, water holes, and lakes all over here and there. Terrance ended up here with us after the roller coasters started showing up."

"But you aren't from around here."

"Not originally. Most of our parents were not from here at all. I, myself, am third generation. Brooke and TwoStep over there, they had a daughter who's fourth generation born here. But that's not the story."

"Oh."

"So here we all are moved to, with new everything. Not a bad thing, just a thing that's new and now we have to figure out how we do things here. You know how it is, things change, we change. Humans like changing things all the time. Did you ever notice that? They just go about changing things over and over and over. I don't think they even bother wondering what happens when they do it." Zed looked off into a distant spot and paused. His thoughts pondering a why that can not be answered. At least by a zebra.

"I spend most of my time staying out of their way in general."

"That makes you a smarter crow than you know." Zed returned to his story telling gaze toward Jack. "Zebras are pragmatic. Did you know that Jack?"

"No. No I did not, Zed."

"Well, we are. Put a group of us together, Grevy's or Grant's, and we'll pragmatically handle our day."

"I see."

"Turtles can't think around corners. Did you know that Jack?"

"No. No I did not, Zed."

"Well, they can't. Further more once they've got themselves stuck in a corner they can't think around, they panic. They get uptight. They become driven to simply go under, over or through a corner. Jack, I've witnessed turtles so stuck in a corner and so determined to unstick themselves they loose their minds. They are simply unaware of their puny physical nature with limited physical abilities to do anything about that corner they are stuck in. It's this misunderstanding that makes them uptight."

"I see."

"So here we are in a new place. New place for us, new corners for Terrence. We pragmatic, he; uptight. Days go by and we zebra figure out our new place. It's larger, with more trees, a deeper bigger pond and paths to herd over. We zebra broke up into two groups to figure things out quicker. I led my group through the flat plains and brush. We kept track of all the tasty bushes and grass spots. We tallied all the shady spots. We noted all the cool spots with good winds for hot days. The other group headed up by Brooke, took the low lands and waterholes. They found two waterholes. They found Terrence in the second one. He was a mess. Brooke attempted to talk him down from his uptightness. While they discussed his uptight, another turtle came out of the water. Barry. Barry and Terrence knew each other from the previous waterhole, which helped. Barry wasn't as uptight as Terrence and joined Brooke in helping Terrence understand the simpler things of turtling.

Brooke and her herd came back with their tallies and memories of cool waters, wet and tasty waterhole greens and a story of five boulders situated not far from the bigger waterhole. You can see that over there, right?"

"Oh yes, yes I do. That seems very accommodating."

"It is, the waterhole is behind them. Privacy is important to zebra. It's easier to be pragmatic when there's privacy."

"I see."

"Terrence and Barry were reasonable in nature. As time went on they were able to compose themselves more pragmatic and less uptight. We zebra prefer being near our waterholes. It's warm here, I think you would agree, Jack."

"Oh, yes! It is warm, quite warm."

"Being near our favored waterhole, behind the boulders, put us all at the mercy of Terrence and Barry, unfortunately."

"Wait, how can that work? You're a herd of zebra, they're just two turtles."

"You see, there you go judging. Zebra are pragmatic and sensitive. We are practically empaths! Our size and glorious stripes hide our very delicate nature. Terrence is a veritable palpating pounding dome of negativity! He's exhausting. Why Brooke can barely stand being around him. You could simply say, "How are you doing today Terrence?" and he'd answer, "Fine." Except for all the things he can't find or get to because he can't think around corners. A zebra would simply stop trying to think around those specific corners knowing change is not coming. But a turtle simply cannot be not uptight."

"I see, pardon me for asking but what does this have to do with who zebras do not listen to?"

"Are you part turtle, Jack? Because that's a very uptight question."

"No. No I'm not but, I see your point."

"Months and years go by as we share our favored waterhole with an uptight turtle and his not as uptight, but may as well be, turtle friend. Every day is the same for these two. So you know how it is Jack. You just stop asking questions, and you stop listening to answers to questions you didn't ask."

"That's a pragmatic solution indeed."

"Yes, we thought so. Years go by and each day we enjoy our waterhole while blocking out the sounds of kvetching turtles. We've gotten good at this Jack. The Grevy's utilize dirt kicking and head shaking. While the Grant's apply small stampede bursts. The noise and ruckus drowns out the turtle complaints quite well."

"I can imagine that to be fruitful."

"One day during a mini stampede burst a few zookeepers were here and witnessed our trying to drown out the turtle's kvetching. I assumed they heard all the negativity as well, and realized that we, zebra, were far too pragmatic and sensitive to endure anymore of all their sorrowed corner sticking."

"Or maybe they thought you were trying to drown the turtles."

Zed stepped back in shock at this accusation. "Zebra are not violent! We are passive observers. But we can only take so much. No matter the zookeeper's thoughts to it all, they did bring a big net and retrieve our uptight turtles and moved them to the flamingo's pond. I say to you now, zebra listen to anyone. Anyone that has anything pragmatically positive to say. We are very good listeners. Greetings Jerry!"

"Hey, Zed. I see you've met Jack."

"Yes, he's quite a good listener. Albeit he does ask more questions than I like to answer."

"That's why we love him, Zed! Hey Jack, let's get lunch."

"Oh! That reminds me, Terrence wants you to get him that burrito thing." Jack was glad to have the burden of remembering to remind Jerry off his back.

"Terrence always wants me to get that burrito thing."

Zed laughed and nodded goodbyes to Jack and Jerry. He led his herd to the boulders in front of their favorite waterhole that no longer contained two uptight turtles. Jack was certain such a change made quite a big difference for the zebras.

Jerry hopped a gust of wind with Jack right behind on the tail breezes. They headed toward the roller coaster filled with screaming humans hanging upside down while being tipped back and forth. Jack couldn't make a lick of sense out of that. The winds grew steady and light as the heat grew into the afternoon. The smell of food grew stronger as the size of the roller coaster grew enormous. Human voices became clearer through all the human screaming. Jerry perched on a roof overlooking a path that weaved it's way around the the roller coaster that went no where. Jack landed next to him and looked up. The roller coaster itself was loud as it roared passed. The screaming humans sounded less frantic and more pleased with themselves. Jack paused a thought. That was a huge thing to make to feel like your flying. Because that's what it looked like. All these screaming pleased humans had their arms up and out while they rushed by in their cars. They were flying. To the best of their inabilities.

Jerry breathed in deep and loud. He looked down on the pathway to see all the walking humans carrying all kinds of foods. You could count on a human to waste what they ate. And you could count on little humans to share what they ate. "Hey Jack, look over there."

Jack pulled his attention from flying humans to look in Jerry's direction.

"See that Jack? You see that little human over there on the bench?"

"Yeah, I do."

"You see what she's doing?"

"She's eating."

"Then so are we. You can always count on a little human to share what they eat. If you like what they share, then you can get as much as you like by acting all ...helpless."

"Helpless?"

"Yes! They are ready to help just about any creature if that creature acts helpless and hungry. I kid you not. Act like you can't feed yourself and they will dump their lunch on your head! Just watch! You gotta see this in action." Jerry flew hard and fast in a straight line to land on the path a few feet in front of the little girl holding a bag of something. Jack watched astonished as Jerry played out lunch.

"Are you watching?"

"Yes! Isn't she going to know you're talking to me?"

"No! They don't think we talk at all. I could stand here yelling at you all day long, and she'll just offer more stuff to eat. They aren't that smart!" Jerry laughed at that last idea and stood with his beak open wide while looking at Jack out of the corner of his eye.

"Aw, little bird, are you hungry?" She shifted herself on the bench and dug deep into her bag to pull out the longest french fry she could find. She leaned forward and tossed it at Jerry's feet. Jerry ate a few bits and looked at the little girl between bites. She smiled. He laughed and grabbed the remaining fry and flew to Jack's side.

"You see how I ate some in front of her? You have to reward them with a look and act like you like what you have, even if you don't. Because you can fly off, spit it out and go back for something different." Jerry divided the remaining fry and handed Jack his share.

"No. No no, let me get my own. Let me try this out."

Jack flew down to the young girl as Jerry had and stood tall. "Hey! Jerry! How's this? Is this right?"

"Yeah. Now yell at me and wait."

"Yell at you and …why am I yelling at you…"

"Aw! Are you a friend of the other bird? Here! Do you want some, too?" The little girl on the bench dug deep for a french fry for Jack. She spoke while hunting for just the right one. "You know you birds are cute. I wish I had a bird like you then I could feed you every day all the time." She tossed Jack his portion. Jack followed Jerry's instructions by eating a few bites while looking at the girl. She laughed. Jack laughed. Jerry landed next to him.

"Okay, here's the beauty part. Don't move, you gotta see this up close. I'm gonna hop around, and you do that too, but don't go too far. See? She's out of those french fries and will ask her mom to share some of her sandwich. Just watch. It happens every time. But you have to wait until the little ones run out of their food." Jack and Jerry bounced and hopped in front of the little girl both crowing and begging.

As Jerry predicted she showed her empty bag to her mother, who handed her the remaining bits of her own lunch wrapped in paper.

Jack and Jerry stopped bouncing and stood still for the toss. The little girl unwrapped her chicken sandwich with care and began tossing chicken and bread to the crows. Jack looked at Jerry. Then the foods. Then the little girl, then back to Jerry. "What is this place!?"

"This, my friend, is where we'll spend our summer."

Jack tasted bits of sandwich. Jerry had the best plans, no matter what state of planning they were in. Jack and Jerry found two more snacks and dessert from a little boy wearing a blue hat sitting under a tree further down the path.

"You ever meet a rhinoceros?"

Jack swallowed the last of his strawberry short cake snack. Where these names came from was a question he needed to ask someone. Rhinoceros, zebra, lion, giraffe …who made this stuff up? "No, I have not, Jerry."

"Good! Let's take a nap until the winds change. Then we can go see Gregory, you'll find him interesting. He's more interesting the cooler the winds get. There's a tree away from all this noise that has a long branch that hangs over a pond. I sleep there most times. The koi fish sing you to sleep."

Koi fish sing?! Add that piece of news to his list of things that need explaining. Jack wiped his beak on the leg of the bench the little boy wearing a blue hat sat on while talking to his father. His father was busy looking at one of those things that never stopped talking. The boy seemed intent on out talking that thing. But so far, he wasn't winning. He father just nodded his head and said things like, "Uh huh. Really? Well that's great!" But he never looked at his son. Just the ceaselessly blaring thing in his hand. Maybe if the father gave his son one of those he would see him better through it.

Jack dismissed the thought. Who would want to look at a picture rather than the real thing? That made no sense at all. Jack waited for Jerry to wipe his beak on the sidewalk surface. Jerry stood straight and called a thank you to the little boy talking to his father not listening.

"Always say thank you, Jack. It's a nice thing to do and I've met the same human twice before. There's a chance of that here. Let's go take a sleep!"

Jack and Jerry set wing to the south. The winds were still slow, too warm, and a hindrance rather than a help. They worked their way up into cooler prevailing air flow. A southerly promise of cooler winds to come. Later. When the sun passed it's arch to begin it's descent into end of day.

*****

The same warm winds that barely moved for Jerry and Jack filled the pine tree overlooking the yellow house where Lisa Douglas and her parrots lived. Todd and Jill sat in the pine tree watching her stand on her deck looking to the sky. "Do you think she's looking for Jack?"

"Of course. We're looking for Jack. So it would make sense she is, too. She is Jack's human."

Jill perched worried and melancholy for Jack's human. They weren't smart, but there were some that were quite kind and loyal. She looked like one of those humans. Jill looked in the direction she heard Jack traveled last in flight, following Jerry into the horizon's hidden truths.

Helen had counseled Jill to be patient not worrying about him. He was a grown crow, taking after his father in flight and fancy. Best to let them chase their ideas to the end and come back to share their results.

Once Edgar had left for two full seasons. He'd gone north to see how far north could go. He'd given Helen a peck on the cheek and leaned into her wing with a promise. I will be back, he said. I will be back with amazing stories and new ideas for us. Edgar didn't notice Helen's disinterest in new ideas. She leaned back against his wing with trust and heartache. Always chasing the things that won't give better answers than those found at home. She believed that truth to her fragile hallow bird bones. Jill listened to her story because listening was comforting.

Edgar left at sunrise the following morning, the winds in his favor. They did not say good bye to each other. Helen told him he could say hello twice, when he got back.

Early Spring broke into Summer and Summer slowly revealed an intent to break free and leave behind it's Fall. As Jill absorbed the words that told the story of Helen's wait, she tried to feel Helen's ache. She tried to experience not knowing where and when the lonely would end. Empathy is a awkward trial. You search the personal experiences in your own mind to match that which most closely resembles the experience of those you wish to empathize. Hers was far too easy to find. She knew this lonely with no defined time or expiration. She knew it well.

"Hey! There's Stiltz! We should see if he knows anything about Jack and Jerry. Stiltz goes where Jerry goes."

Jill pulled herself from Helen's story running in her mind.

Stiltz was wandering the shade along the fence line of the yellow house. The grass was longer there, and the chance for bugs to eat more promising.

"Yes! Let's!" Before Todd could answer she left the branch to glide down to the shade Stiltz hunted. "Hi Stiltz!"

"Good day to you, Jill. He's fine. He's at the place with the genius giraffe and interesting rhinoceros." Stiltz didn't bother looking up. He was on top of a group of grubs. He could feel their panic under his toes.

Todd plopped to the left of Stilz with a bluster. The long grass poked his wing feathers, and a moth flew into his face escaping the blitz of landing crow. He was left to jump again, spit, cough, and shake his head hoping the moth wasn't already in his mouth. Todd did not eat moths. He drew the bug line on moths.

Jill watched his struggle against a moth long gone. She shook her head. How can so many crows be so bad at crow living? She looked back to Stiltz.

"Thank you, Stiltz. We are worried for him. What's out there sounds quite, different."

"Different isn't bad and genius giraffes are handy! I can take you to him you know. You could see what he's seeing and then you'll understand that different isn't that unusual."

Stiltz felt for her. Crow family depend on strict rule following. It struck Stiltz long ago that if one murder of crow would just agree to be different in a different place, that could help them all. But to this point Stiltz only knew two crow willing to try; Edgar and Jerry. He'd add Jack to that list. Once Jack realized what he didn't need to know.

"No. No thank you, Stiltz. I couldn't possibly. It's just not what a crow does. You know I'm a good crow."

"I do, Jill! You are a fine crow. A crow any neighbor or murder member can count on in a pinch. My offer stands as long as Jack is gone. I am happy to fly you in the right direction."

"You are so kind Stiltz, you are practically crow."

Stiltz laughed trying to shrug off a blush. He liked Jill. A kind crow he knew would only say what she meant.

"What's over there where Jack is, anyway?" Todd spoke over the moment. He assumed all along Jack was fine. What he didn't understand was why a crow of his caliber would leave to go somewhere else for whatever there may not be here. No reasons at all. He just left. What crow does that without knowing?

"What's over there is easier to understand while you look at it. How can I describe a genius giraffe, roller coasters or uptight turtles. I can't. You just have to see it all. You should see it all. I'll take you there. My offer stands for you as well, Todd."

"Giraffe, roller coasters …do you make up these words as you go along or did Jerry make them up first?"

"No need to get snotty, Todd. They are real words for real creatures and things. You just haven't seen them and you don't know. I've seen them. I've had a conversation with some of them. I know."

Todd lost interest in points made thanks to the annoying ants crawling over his claws in the tall grass. He shook a foot to loosen their crawly claws attempting to climb past his knee. He loosened the last ant's grip as he took flight.

Ant was no more than a Stiltz height from the ground when he let go, but ant knew the distance would take a bit. He curled into a ball to soften the landing back into the grass. Unfurled his abdomen and straightened his antenna after landing and looked up to the crow disappearing into the glare of the sky. Being an ant was taxing.

Ant found his fellow colony members back where he'd first started, where the grubs had dug. If a colony can find easy starts to projects, an ant will take advantage to save on frustration. Grub diggings are an excellent short cut to excavating foods and such. A good grub dug hole can save a full day's work. That's quite a bit of angst avoided.

Moving the colony nearer to the yellow house was also a great short cut. When he first heard the idea from the army members he wasn't so sure. Moving the queen and the colony into digs not yet dug was dangerous. The good news was the find of an abandoned termite tunnel system. Termites build systems waiting for a good piece of wood or dead tree to go to later. The move closer to the house went smoother than most expected and the queen had nothing but good things to say all around.

Another great short cut was the human in the yellow house that fed the ducks and crows and ibis. Because ducks, crows, and ibis rarely finish their meals. Harvesting leftover bits and niggles became a simple process of ground traveling under the shade of the lawn. Between the grub, the termites, and the human an ant's tedium decreased substantially.

Ant joined the transfer line of his fellow members carrying a bit of green something or other. He balanced it between his mandibles while resting the length of it over is head and down his back. No one spoke because no one had an empty mouth to speak with, but all followed with perfectly timed scrambling feet.

Each ant dropped into the entry hole leading to the tunnel that led to the food storage bank. There, ants worked tirelessly chewing and working all the found foods into ant breads to be dispersed at breakfast, lunch, and dinner times. Since ants worked in shifts the kitchen was always serving someone. He was three members away from entering back into his colony's tunnel system to drop his find off at the food bank.

Being an ant was satisfying. Each had their job to complete and each job's completion was equally important. He dropped into the hole and progressed forward behind his fellow members. The darkness closed in. Ants don't need light to travel, or make progress. The temperature changed along with the humidity, which was a welcome change for any ant. He followed his precedent ants coming into the food chamber at a quick shuffle pace. There's no time for chit chat for an ant. He simply dropped his green morsel at the feet of one of the ant cooks and continued the quick shuffle behind his fellow ants to head back out into the sun light to be greeted by three grouse, on lunch break.

*****

From the top of trees things at the bottom of trees look small. You get used to it after a while. That first few days is a little off-putting though. Jack and Jerry were at the very top of the very tip of the very center tallest branch of an old pine tree. The older the tree, the taller. This was an old tree. Looking down the rhinoceros looked unimpressive. Jack rode the swaying branch along with Jerry, both thinking on thoughts not at all related.

Jerry's concerns lay in whether to eat dinner at the new roller coaster or the old one. Jack's concern lay at the feet of the beasts below. He knew the sizing upgrade that would take place when he and Jerry flew down the height of the pine tree. He also knew he'd never spoke to a rhinoceros before, and hadn't a clue as to what to talk about with them. They seemed hard to impress, even from this height. Jerry and Jack came to their conclusions out loud at the same time. "I suppose lunch at the new roller coaster will get the newer tastes." intertwined with, "I suppose I can start with a grand hello and see where things lead from there." leaving "I suppose I can start lunch with a grand hello at the new roller coaster and see where the newer tastes lead from there." Which made as clear a statement as any other they'd shared.

Simultaneously jumping off the tree and sailing toward the rhinoceros they nodded heads in agreement. Jerry landed on a boulder situated next to the rhinoceros.

"Hi Rhinosaurus!"

"Rhinoceros, the "o" is short, not long."

"Huh?"

Jerry landed on a shorter boulder to the right of Jack. He saw Jack's look of confusion.

"Rhine AH ceros. Not Rhino Saurus."

"Well Conrad said it was pronounced …" before he could finish his defense of pronunciation, one more correction came.

"Never mind. Just call me Gregory."

"Oh! Yes, I've heard you do have a good name."

Jack shook out his feathers to get them to lay better. The winds were picking up for an evening rain. He turned a bit in place to face them. "Excuse me, Gregory, if I might." He felt it better to ask permission to have a conversation considering this Gregory rhino was as large as his boulder.

"You might."

"I do have a question, and mind you, you are the first rhinoceros I've met (Jack did his best to pronounce the word with a short "o"). You look like you were meant to knock things down. Is that what you do? Knock things down?" Jack froze. He realized that question sounded far better inside his head rather than outside. Jerry's face agreed.

"You look like you were meant to not know things." Gregory took a step to the right toward a clump of grass.

"Most days I feel that way, yes."

A conversational stand off took place. Jerry stayed on his high ground staying out of it. Jack stood crow eye to rhino eye, while they both waited to see who had the better answer to each other without saying a word.

Rhinoceros are not only made to knock things over, but they are made to stay put. A rhino that doesn't want to move will not be moved. Being heavy and short legged their center of gravity serves both purposes equally. Rhino tend to prefer to stay put, in groups, standing on tasty grounds and mounds.

Gregory was a stay put kind of rhino by nature. His sister, Sandra was more of a knock things down rhino. The three new younger rhinos had no idea what their preferences were, spending half the day knocking down small boulders into smaller and the other half staying put.

Gregory sensed they were better at knocking things down, but who's to say what youth will reveal at the coming of age. Gregory knew a rhino once who preferred nothing more than digging ditches. He would spend all his free time scuffing the soil to reveal the softer areas perfect for digging. He would dig until the ibis showed up to see if he'd unearthed any grubs. His name was Ken, if he remembered right. Come to think of it, he'd not seen Ken since last he'd met Stiltz, that untrusting ibis. That was the way of things, dinner party guests stay as long as the guests they are interested in stay on. Gregory was still staring at Jack.

"This a new friend of yours Jerry?" His gaze stayed put as well as the rest of him.

"New to you, not to me. This is Jack. He normally has questions to go along with his greetings. Just so you know."

"I've gathered. What are you doing over at this end of the park? It's close to dinner, you don't eat rhino dinners, or do you now?"

"Oh no, not yet. All due respect, rhino tastes aren't for me."

"No offence taken, crow tastes aren't for me. Last time you bragged it was about a lunch you'd foraged for yourself. A rotten turtle egg if I remember right. Which I always do. Remember right, that is."

Jack's laughter escaped before he could control it. Jerry bragged about that turtle egg? To a rhino? Jack snickered along with his thoughts. I don't even know what a rhino is all the way yet, and I'd have known rotten turtle eggs were not on it's preferred dinner list. Jack shook his head finishing up a light giggle.

Gregory seemed pleased a crow would laugh at his joke. Jerry hadn't decided whether he'd laugh with or at himself. Neither choice felt fruitful. "Tell Jack what you told me last year. Remember? We were talking about traveling and seeing new things and not asking questions all the time."

"No we were not. We were discussing your need to arrive unannounced only to speak incessantly to me about those things I had no need to know about in the first place."

Jack glanced Jerry's way wondering if this too would be an appropriate time to laugh. These rhinoceros were amusing. Gregory waited for an appropriate response and received nothing. "Jack it is unfortunate we've met at the hands of Jerry. I'm sure we would have gotten on with our own conversation without all this brouhaha. Do you hail from Jerry's area of home?"

"Yes, we're from the same murder."

"Ah! I see, friends not family, then."

"Yes. He's been generous with his time to show me this side of the world. This is the first time I've left our home at all. I have to say, this has all been an experience I won't forget."

"Will you be staying awhile or is this just a day trip?"

Jerry jumped into the conversation. Sitting quiet and still was not his skillset. "We're staying the summer. Jack needs to figure some things out before committing to a girl."

"Hey! I'm not figuring girl committing at all! I'm just trying to figure out the why of it all."

Gregory began rubbing his ribs against the larger boulder. Thinking and scratching went hand in hand for a rhinoceros. Jerry swayed with the boulder as Gregory's weight had it's way with the monolith. Jack could feel his boulder being knocked against. Deep beneath both boulders napped a ground squirrel named Harry.

Ground squirrels don't mind being woken by unknown events. Most ground squirrels are agreeable to handling the unknown arrival of whatever. What does rub a ground squirrel the wrong way is being woken for no reason at all. This was just such a moment. He could hear Gregory's low voice reverberating through the ground filling his den with the familiar tenor of a rhinoceros full of himself and all his ideas. That too, was not a good enough reason to wake Harry. There was no solution to the matter but to climb his way out of bed and up the tunnel hidden between two boulders that were now castanets without a beat.

Harry raised his head above ground level to see a rhinoceros foot blocking his way out. How could one rhino be this much trouble? He should have set up a den in the kangaroo gardens. They had the best conversations; very few. Harry pushed and squeezed between boulders and out the back rather than battle a calloused rhino foot.

"Why is not as important as when. For example; when I eat is more important than why I ate. If I forget the when the why doesn't matter. You see how that works don't you?"

Harry decided to stomp his way around the smaller boulder to come round to face Gregory. He'd lost too many friends to stomping behind rhinos.

Harry finished his approach by placing his left rear paw down with great fury. Fury reserved only for ground squirrel woken early. "What gives Gregory! We had a deal, a simple deal between you up there and me down here."

"Harry, this is Jack, he's visiting from afar and we were just debating deeper matters of life."

"It takes this much noise to debate deeper matters of life? Seriously?"

"Well it may have been more the itch on my ribs than the matters of life conversation. This boulder makes a marvelous rib scratcher."

Jack continued to watch Harry, hoping he'd relax and say hello to Gregory's introduction. Harry had other ideas not including meeting any one new. He stood, arms crossed, feet apart staring Gregory down, eyes to horn. Gregory smiled with little show of reflected angst. He waited for Harry to wear out.

Ground squirrels wear out quickly, unlike their cousins in the trees. A ground squirrel can display angst for 15 minutes, if they've had a nap. A tree squirrel, without a nap, can go all afternoon displaying angst, giddiness or any number of elevated emotions. Gregory knew this through experience. He waited. Harry's chest heaved with shallow breaths waiting for Gregory to admit that everything going on was wrong, and an apology would be offered immediately. Harry waited.

Jack recognized this moment. He'd been a participant long ago with Todd. He and Todd agreed they would not be doing any foraging until they investigated a tree that had fallen down in the storm the night before. They had agreed.

Jack trusting Todd had gone to the fallen tree at the time agreed only to find Todd had already foraged all the good bits that had been blown off the tree.

He found Todd standing next to a broken bird feeder and it's spilled contents. Todd said nothing. Jack said nothing. They looked at each other frozen in time. Jack waited for excuses and Todd waited for Jack's speech about agreements. Neither was willing to offer their version of the next step.

Harry broke down first. He wore himself out in his own head. Gregory watched Harry's arms fall to the little squirrel's side and his breath slow it's pace. For all his bluster, Gregory worried one day little Harry would die of a heart attack on the very spot he waited for his satisfaction. It wouldn't be right to drop dead waiting for satisfaction.

Jerry interrupted the silence and most likely an excellent comment by a patient rhinoceros. "Well, I see you two have things to talk about. We've got to get some dinner and get back to our roost before night. We'll leave you two to it!" Jerry hopped onto Jack's boulder and shouldered Jack into a free fall into flight off the boulder. They both took wing heading toward the last snack of the day.

As Jack and Jerry became floating spots in an ever darkening sky Gregory smiled. Harry shrugged his shoulders. "Have you seen the acorns on the other side of my fence?"

"Yes, I have Gregory, I ought to gather those for later now that you mention them. Did you want a few?"

"Yes, I would Harry. We should share a snack and discuss that agreement I so selfishly forgot."

"No. No you weren't being selfish, we all forget things. I could have been more patient actually."

Gregory shrugged his shoulders. Harry smiled. That's the way of friends. You wouldn't be friends if you didn't already know about these things. What makes you friends is the knowing part. What makes you best friends is knowing and not caring as much about it as you care for your friend.

*****

Jack slipped inside Jerry's stream following him to dinner. Neither started a conversation but rather enjoyed the nature of flight. The wind rushing over the feathers, the whoosh of air past earholes. Feeling the pressure change to find the boost of warm air to gain the height or loose it for landing. Done right, a crow could meditate from destination to destination.

"There! Jack you see it!?"

Jack took in the view growing in size. They were back where the humans were thick in groups. They all carried foods. They all ate and drank and took seats at tables and chairs. There were places up and down the pavement as far as the eye could see. Places serving foods of every smell Jack had ever smelled. Most of the smells were new, but familiar in nature. Popcorn wasn't new, but large balls of popcorn sticky and sweet were. Hotdogs weren't new. But hotdogs on sticks covered in cornbread was new. Nachos, burgers, pizza and salads. Those were not new. Jerry landed on a tall wall. Jack came in to his right. They looked down at a smorgasbord.

"I don't know what to say about any of this …"

"Neither did I the first seven times."

"Where do you start?"

"I've found starting in front of a kid on a bench is the best place to start. It's an even better place to start if there are two kids together, sharing."

Jack looked down and saw three children seated on a bench laughing. They were sharing their dinners with each other. Jerry watched the same scene. "Two girls and a boy. Girls are always willing to share. One boy is willing to share because girls are there. One boy alone will share. Two boys may share after throwing the first piece at your head. Three boys will not share. And never ever approach more than three boys together, alone, ever. Nothing good or good tasting can come from it. You can approach any number of girls at any time to share. Unless it's a birthday party. That's when things get weird."

"How do you know it's a birthday party specifically?"

"The girls are screaming and running. There's a table with no food, but colorful boxes and bags. There are adults wondering around drinking from afar. They seem fearful as well if you ask me. And sooner or later they set desert on fire, sing a song of birthdays and give the flaming cake to the birthday girl."

"Whoa. That sound dangerous."

"Exactly."

"Well that's a shame, seems there's food gone to waste then."

"I've found it's best to wait until late afternoon, when the adults bring three bags of garbage to the outside can. Two are full of colored paper, paper plates, cups and wads of wet paper towels. One bag has all you can eat birthday foods.

I've noticed the birthday girl successfully blows out the flaming desert cake. To get leftovers of that you have to go to bag two, where the plates are…"

"Hardly seems worth it."

"I have to agree."

Jerry landed in front of the bench holding the three children sharing french fries, two hamburgers, and one hotdog. They didn't notice him. They were too busy dividing up the three meals of food to share equally. They were too busy laughing and talking about roller coasters.

"Jack! Get down here! We need to team up on this one!"

Jack flew down out of the tree to Jerry's right. "What's the problem?"

"I landed too early. They're divvying up the food yet and talking about roller coasters. It'll take two of us to get through all that hullabaloo. So let's do what I like to call the high five. I'll go first. Do what I do but land on the back of bench." Jerry bolted straight up, cawed loud and landed on the girl's summer hat that rested over her knee. Jack froze.

Who does that? Jerry was sure to die now. You don't just land on them! That's not how they work. You have land near them, caw and wait. No one gets hurt. Jerry lived in the danger zone. The little girl put a french fry in her mouth and looked at Jerry with a smile. Jack cawed a goodbye and waited for the inevitable.

"Highlo little bird. You are a cute little birdie all black and little aren't you?"

Jerry lowered his head and raised it standing straight, tilted his head and whistled. Jack paid no attention to the boy near him trying to hand him a french fry. He was mesmerized by Jerry's skillset. Acting like a baby bird! He'd never thought of that idea. Of course the little girl wouldn't know he wasn't a baby bird because she was not a crow! What would she know?

"Highlo little bird. You look hungry do you want a french fry? You can have one of mine little black bird baby bird."

She gently held out a french fry while Jerry acted skittish. His acting did not include refusing. Jack's attention turned to the french fry floating in front of his own face.

"Hey! Bird! You want this or not? Your friend is going to get all of Katie's. You can have mine."

Jack looked past the french fry to the hand and followed it down to the arm and then face that owned the arm. The boy wore a big smile, and a look that asked, are you stupid or what? Jack grabbed the fry and cawed a thank you.

Jerry stayed on the hat to eat, Jack stayed on the bench. The two girls and boy spent the remaining lunch time sharing french fries with Jack and Jerry. The children discussed where they would go if they could fly. They all agreed flying would be a great thing to do.

*****

The sun skimmed the horizon over the lake across the way. Jack and Jerry were perched in a weeping willow tree. They were behind the swaying drapery of branches, secure near the trunk, on the thicker branches leading out to the draping ends.

If you didn't know they were there, you would not see them. Half the sun dipped into the lake as the koi fish began their song. Jack looked down to see the spectacle and hear their music.

Koi sing with water. The droplets playing against each other and sounding again as they return to the pond's collective. Koi mouth the surface from below looking for last remnants of food or careless insects floating. This music requires a multitude of fish to create. If only one or two koi fish are feeding for the last time it's water splashing. But if there are dozens of fish of varying sizes, each koi creates their own note. And each note added upon another creates a symphony of gurgles, splishes, splashes, and droplets.

The sun slipped into the lake leaving it's final glow cast back into the sky. Orange slashes of disturbed water marked it's entry point. Jerry was fast asleep, beak tucked. Jack, amazed by the splendor of sounds and sights, fought his sleepy eyes to take in all that he'd never known. The koi's colors matched the oranges dancing their way into the darkness. The insects offered a closing symphony to the sun's final orange dissolving into the darkest of purples ahead. There was nothing to see, and every thing to hear at this day's end. Jack allowed his eyes to close, and hoped somehow sleep would not come too quick cutting off the music of life with no human competing.

They were so loud, humans. Their caterwauling blocked out the natural world's orchestra. Jack held cicadas in high regard. They were hidden songsters. They left a part of themselves hanging on trees as a signature to their evening's concert. At least that's what he was told, and what he heard summer evenings. As the human race faded away nature came forward with a vengeance of song and sound. Birds randomly called into the night. Insects grew fearless knowing they had the protection of night surrounding them. Rustling leaves. Koi lapping and quietly circling in the pond. A frog croaked. A toad answered in kind. The frog called back to make sure the toad didn't get the last word. Birds called. Insects increased their volume to get a word in edgewise over the toads and frogs. Leaves rustled allowing the mice egress to the ground to forage for the bits and bites left behind by the noisy humans now long gone. Koi fighting over a bug, most likely not paying attention to his whereabouts, created waves in the pond that lapped at the shore that disturbed the frog that croaked his disapproval who then had to listen to the retort of a toad he'd thought had finished his opinion earlier.

Jack realized sleeping in this spot would be problematic. These creatures were deafening as a whole. He rustled his own leaves to find a comfortable position. He let his mind wander over all the sounds as he would fly over the tree tops. Sleep approached gently. As gently as the cicada situating himself above Jack. It was time to sing loud to find his mate.

An adult male cicada of a certain type has a call of 120 decibels. An adult male cicada of a certain other type has a call so high only dogs can hear them. Jack's new cicada neighbor was the former. Ken had no intention of rattling his neighbors with 120 decibels. That would be rude. He'd keep it down below 100. Ninety-eight seemed fair and appropriate for the job at hand. His mother instructed him years ago that a woman does not want a man that talks over everyone else. A good woman prefers a good man that can listen. He would call at 98 decibels for three minutes at a time, then listen for five minutes. Striking a balanced conversational pace. He was by every measure, a thoughtful cicada.

Jack's left foot reacted to Ken's first note.

The foot muscles released their grip in sheer terror as the claws attached to them retreated north to hide in the feathers above. Jack's leg muscles contracted in agreement at the same time. Jack's brain kicked in informing the right leg and foot that under no circumstances were they joining in all this reactionary overreacting. Jack's eyes popped open and his head twitched left, right, up, and down seeking information. What was making that noise and where was it making it? Jack's left foot and leg decided to pull it together and gut out the current goal of locating the sound rather than hiding. He regained his footing.

Ken checked his internal clock to see how long he had to go with this first call. One minute. He continued the rhythmic buzzing hum that most ladies found enticing. And one special lady would find irresistible. All in all making the sound was a pleasant exercise. There was a full body vibration a cicada could enjoy.

The darkness was not helping Jack find the noise maker. But the noise itself proclaimed the location to be close. So close that thing could be on his head. And then it stopped. The missing 98 decibels left room for the surrounding nature to have it's say. Jack widened his eyes and slowly gazed from left to right allowing his retina to find the light available. Ken stirred in his spot relocating one clawed foot just a bit lower and another clawed foot just a bit higher facilitating a better sounding mechanism in the coming second round of calling. Jack heard the claws just as his eyes found sight of the owner of the claws.

"All that noise came out of you!?" Jack hadn't seen a cicada. He'd only heard them. He'd always assumed they were the size of a healthy raccoon, and better at hiding. What he saw couldn't be the producer of all that racket. It didn't add up.

"This is what I do. It's my job. I'm good at it and I'm not apologizing for my skills. You should be aware that I am actually keeping it down and holding back a bit. I could peel the bark off this tree if I wanted. I am, if you can't notice, being quite polite."

"Isn't there another way to accomplish whatever it is you're attempting up there?"

"No."

"Are you sure?"

"Yes."

"Quite sure?"

"Very."

"Well, what is it that you're doing anyway?"

"I am, if you must know, letting the ladies know I am here."

"How long will that take, do you think?"

"I haven't a clue how long. This is my first attempt."

Jack had a decision to make. If this cicada was good at any of this, there would be lady cicadas flying in for a look see shortly. If this cicada was bad at any of this, he would by virtue of his own confidence not give up. In either case this tree had suddenly lost it's charm.

"Psst! Jerry!"

He'd consult Jerry on moving away from the tree of enticements. Surely he'd not slept through all this buzz humming woman calling business. He raised his whispering voice for effect.

"Psst! JERRY!"

Ken interrupted. "Will you be pssting all night? I can't tell what all that will do for my work here. I can't see good ladies wanting to put up with some crow pssting in the dark. You are cramping my style bird."

Jack perched in silence. Jerry was asleep to the world. This cicada was insulting. And by the looks of things the sun was hours away. "I don't appreciate the tone you're taking. I was here first you know."

"No. No you weren't I was at this tree before you. I've been at this tree, just 6 months short of 17 years. This tree and this night are my destiny!"

(Ken's 5th grade teacher, Miss Dornbury, had noted on Ken's middle school report card his tendency toward the over dramatic.)

*****

Jack woke to mad scrambling of claws detaching and reattaching to the bark of the tree. This morning in the breaking light of today, he knew who was making the noise. It had to be the cicada. He glanced up and took in the site of cicadas copulating in the glow of dawn. Tragically their ritual was no where near as romantic as the idea of a glowing dawn.

Jack's beak gapped. He wasn't a stalker or gawker, but the site of copulating cicada left quite a lot to understand. First, they were backed up into each other rather than the general one on top of the other sort of copulating. Second, she seemed to direct him, which isn't wrong. More power to the female and all. But he didn't seem at all comfortable with the process and he also seemed lost as how to give up control. So it was more of a struggling event. She seemed perturbed. He seemed shocked she was perturbed.

"Left!"

"What?"

"LEFT. Move left."

"Well, why should we do that if we go right then …"

"LEFT!"

"You don't have to yell at me like that Doreen."

"Your right! MY left!"

"Well, calm down. This shouldn't be this complicated if we go …"

"Ken, why did you invite me over if you had no intention of listening to me in the first place?"

"I listened for 5 minutes! What do you want from me woman!?"

"Your sperm! And honestly I'm not so sure it's that important anymore."

"I didn't climb a tree after 16 and half years for this abuse you know."

"LEFT!"

Jack shrunk down and stopped looking at the pair. They had become embarrassing for the whole tree. He looked down to watch the koi sing and feed on the small things that had fallen onto the water's surface over night. A shadow passed before him and disappeared above his view. A rough scrape, scrambling claws and silence followed. Jerry dropped onto Jack's branch with two disemboweled cicadas in his mouth.

"OH MY CROW you ate Ken and Doreen! Why did you eat Ken and Doreen!?" Jack fell back against the main trunk of the tree shocked. He'd just seen them sexing it up over an argument and now they hung lifeless in Jerry's beak. Doreen still had the look of frustration at Ken on her face. Jerry swallowed before laughing.

"Mr. and Mrs. Hors d'oeuvre were delicious! Why you didn't eat Ken and shut him up last night was beyond me. I lost sleep because you didn't eat him."

"Are you saying Doreen could still be alive if I had? Are you pinning her death on me, like I had something to do with any of this, Jerry!?"

(Jack's 4th grade teacher, Miss Bondango, had noted on Jack's elementary school report card his tendency toward the over dramatic.)

*****

Jack traveled through summer and into early autumn with ease.

Each day brought new confidence to a place in time that became less new. He stopped asking the whys in July. His habit of worrying at night ended in August. By September he was traveling alone and meeting up with Jerry for lunches or naps.

Seasons change with the smallest of increments in Florida. Summer felt quite a bit like Fall which felt pretty much like Winter. Spring was the only season that could bring drastic changes, for a very short amount of time. The difference between Summer and Fall was the sun's path and time spent in the sky. You had to be aware though. It was a subtle change. Jack learned as a fledgling to watch the insects. They went to bed earlier, and they were mostly mosquitoes. Grass moths were ending their life cycles. Crickets tended to slow down and stay in the dark spaces. Dragonfly and butterfly were gone onto their travels elsewhere. The Fall was full of annoying bugs and void of the interesting ones. Jack found himself at Conrad's place more often than not. He and Conrad would stay behind the boulders quietly talking about the world and it's whys. Conrad was genius. There was no debating that fact. The seclusion and their friendship proved to be Jack's most prized moments.

"Will you be heading back to your flock with the Winter approaching?" Conrad slowly chewed lunch. The zoo folk had brought in fresh greens and branches to replace those that were drying in the seasonal changes. He chewed with his eyes closed most times. Conrad lived in the moment. He gave what he was doing his full attention. A giraffe didn't want to miss details. Details are easily missed if you don't pay attention. He chewed, eyes closed, waiting for Jack to consider his question.

"I think I'll be staying until the winter temperatures come.

Jerry says the human population at the roller coasters gets bigger when Fall becomes really Fall and Winter promises to show up. I can only imagine how much great food will be around then."

Conrad chewed. He looked down at his friend on the fence. He was a good bird. Smart. Reliable it seemed. Curious and an excellent listener. He asked good questions, too. Conrad appreciated good questions. "More of the same seems rather plain."

Jack shot a look up to his genius friend. His words were packed full, every time. Seven words held the world in it's grasp. More of the same. There was a thing to think on. He'd left his flock and home because it had become more of the same. He stayed long enough for this place to be more of the same.

"Is that it then? No matter where you go, in the end it turns into more of the same?" He blinked waiting for a genius answer.

Conrad swallowed. He tilted his head and lowered it a bit with an arched neck providing the angle necessary. Giraffe necks are built strong and flexible. They only look stuck.

"Jack, no matter where you go, you are always there. The more of the same isn't where you are, it's how you see things when you're there."

Jack stood taller on his feet. As tall as a crow could get on crow feet. He looked into Conrad's eyes. Conrad's eyelashes tickled his forehead feathers. "Conrad how do you know everything?"

"I don't. I know what needs knowing, and I know what doesn't need knowing. This saves quite a bit of time."

Jack lowered himself back onto the fence. Conrad stood tall again. He smiled down knowing he wouldn't see his good crow friend again. Which he also knew was the way of things. A crow would crow to the best of their abilities, in the end. "I need to go back into the sunshine to warm my knees and let the humans wave at me Jack. The little ones need to know we're more than what they are told. Some know this naturally. Others don't until they can look you in the eyes."

Conrad walked back out in front of the boulders. Jack heard the laughter and calls of the children. Jack admired the walk of a giraffe. Watching Conrad stroll throughout his world was a beautiful sight. Giraffes walk as if they're on a cloud. They don't seem to impact the ground, but rather sink into their feet with each step. Their long legs bend to extend just the length necessary to softly lay their foot against the ground. If you didn't know better, which he did, you would think giraffe feet were slippers. He thoroughly enjoyed watching Conrad be a giraffe. Because Conrad enjoyed being a giraffe. His happy state of giraffe was obvious. Conrad knew who he was and was happy to do Conrad to the best of his ability. He was the best Conrad he could be, happily.

*****

"We know Jack!" Petra and Seta sang their chorus with smiles to match. Stiltz looked up under what eyebrows an ibis possessed. He'd forgotten to tell Jill about the twins propensity to talk at the same time while saying the same words. Jill looked at him in return. She hitched her head toward the twins and shrugged her shoulders. Stiltz could only shrug back in confirmation, yes. Apologies for not letting you know about such a state of affairs. Jill took a deep breath and smiled. She looked at the twins and thought, how close two sisters must be that they know what the other will say. "That wasn't my question ladies. I asked if you knew where he was, now, today."

Ardon the egret didn't know much more than the twins. Although he offered 20 minutes of philosophical thoughts about the matter. She returned her thoughts to the twins at hand and worked up a bigger, friendly smile.

"We don't know where he is now, today. We didn't know where he was yesterday, either. Most likely we won't know anything tomorrow, unless he stops by, but we doubt it. Don't we?" They looked into each other's eyes with sincere sisterly love.

"Well thank you anyway. I don't want to keep you from your feeder. We'll be on our way then."

"Thank you for asking!"

Jill looked at Stiltz. They've only been traveling for an hour or two. She'd only asked three creatures and felt she'd been at it all day. It was like talking to Jerry. Friendly and open with so many ideas not related to the subject at hand. It's all a bit overwhelming to someone with less ideas.

"Let's try Gregory, for a rhinoceros he's precise!"

Jill found herself wanting to ask what a rhinoceros was and why one would not necessarily be precise. Stiltz took flight heading into the winds that carried Jack and Jerry on their own journey before. Jill hopped into the winds to join him reminding herself to ask Stiltz to explain the idea of an imprecise rhinoceros.

Petra looked at Seta in shock and dismay. "We know where Jerry is though. Do you think she wanted to know that? No, no certainly she would have asked if she had but she didn't." The best thing about being able to know what your sister will say and saying it at the same time is the compressed precise conversation taking half the time. They went back to their feeder of songbird seed.

Back before GPS and cellphones, it should be noted here for the human readers, if one were searching for another friend your best bet was to go to all the places you both would go to at some point or another. Once there it would prove fruitful to ask anyone within shouting distance about the location of your friend. You could triangulate a one mile radius of probable location with this exercise. Historically anyone over the age of 33 would not do this, but rather suggest to anyone interested in locating a misplaced friend that they probably didn't want to be found anyway. Leaving plenty of daylight to do other things.

Jill's struggle lay in the fact that neither she nor Stiltz traveled to any of these places or creatures together with Jack. Stiltz would run into Jack on occasion when they both randomly picked the same place and creature to visit. This search was looking for information from individuals who knew Jack and with that information gathered, create understanding of Jack's habits leading to his whereabouts. They landed on a large boulder in the middle of tall grasses, short trees and sandy ground. Jill viewed the answer to her currently unasked question.

Stiltz flapped his wings "Good afternoon Gregory!"

Gregory tipped an ear hello. Jill perched in awe at an enormous, grey, precise, rhinoceros.

"Stiltz! I see you are collecting crows. Jerry was here just an hour ago, with little to say of course. I had to carry the full conversation until he remembered lunch."

"Jerry will always be Jerry. Jack wasn't with him?"

"Oh no. Jack comes and goes on his own these days. Now there is a crow that can hold a conversation. I look forward to his visits. Last time we had a riveting debate on social benefits of helping turtles relax."

"What was your conclusion?"

"It's not possible. Therefore the time and efforts expended wouldn't return much to society as a whole. Best to leave them alone in all their angst."

"I see. The simplest answer tends to be the correct one. This is Jill."

"Jill. It is nice to meet you."

"It's marvelous to meet you Gregory! I have never met a precise rhinoceros before. What a grand moment for me."

"Precise? Why thank you for such kind words. I like to fancy myself a rigorous rhinoceros."

"Commendable Gregory. I'm looking for Jack specifically. He's been gone quite a long time from his flock. I'd hoped to find him and make sure he's well."

"I have no idea where he would be today, but I can say three days ago he was well."

"He's quite well right now over at the roller coaster's edge a little while ago, too!" The voice came from a boulder. Or Jill so thought. There was no body attached to a voice coming from the very crevice of the two boulders meeting under her feet. She looked to Gregory for clarity. This was his boulder after all.

Gregory took a few steps following a lovely line of tall uneaten grass. "That's Harry. His tunnel ends under the boulder you stand on. He can be helpful at times. Not precise mind you, but helpful."

"I don't have to be precise! I only have to be close!" He stuck his head out from between the boulders, his head framed in tall grass a rhinoceros can not reach. "Hello Jill Crow. Hi Stiltz!"

"Harry. How's things under ground?"

"Quite good. I've finished excavating under the hotdog place. Dinner is easier now."

"Congratulations on that success. So, you've seen Jack at the roller coaster today? I take it you finished that excavation as well."

"Oh yes, I completed that portion last Spring." Harry climbed out from under the boulders, brushing off the soil from his knees. He checked his backside for presentability. "He was napping in that tree behind the bench. I didn't bother him. He looked like he was busy digesting. Far be it from me to bother a creature when they are digesting. It's just plain rude."

Jill startled a bit and considered that simple truth. She'd always known ground squirrels to be rational, but this Harry was downright thoughtful.

"Harry can you point us in the right direction?"

Harry looked up at Jill, hands on hips. This one didn't know what a roller coaster was, just like Jack didn't so long ago. Crows need to get out more. He lifted on arm and pointed far off to the east. Jill's gaze followed his pointed paw.

She took in the site of a roller coaster topping a long row of trees. Tall trees from the looks of them. How tall was this roller coaster and what did it do over there? No matter, if Jack was there, that's where she wanted to be.

Jill and Stiltz said their goodbyes and thank you taking off into the eastern moving breezes. They waned now in the afternoon's heat. She pressed down with her wings letting the winds know she would not accept anything less than fluid flight.

*****

It's said the grass is always greener on the other side. The other side of what is the question left behind in the sentiment. The other side of what you know is that answer. Jack woke up under the thick foliage of a convenient crepe myrtle. The tree was hidden away among a compact group of punk trees. He'd found it by accident. His neighbors, a family of woodpeckers, kept to themselves. Most days they were busy hunting out all the insects hidden inside myriad of bark layers a punk tree offered.

Jack faded into the dark recesses of his crepe, falling into a nap surrounded by green leaves. Napping here was a better choice than the tree overlooking the bench in front of the roller coaster. There were times human screams could crawl right up a crow's spine rattling his brain like a dried up gourd.

The woodpeckers were out and about finding their own lunch, the punk trees didn't vibrate with their bug hunting. He made his was out from the center of the tree to perch on an outer exposure to see what there was to see.

"Are they gone?"

Jack had become comfortable with random voices coming from unknown spaces. His travels and time spent here had calmed his need to not so much know things, but rather, accept things.

"They who?" He spoke into the winds not seeking to find the voice's owner, but rather clarity to their question.

"The woodpeckers you fool! Who else would I be talking about? Are they gone?"

Jack crackled a chuckle and looked up to find a snail attached to the underside of a leaf hanging just inches in front of him.

"Yes snail, they are gone for now. I haven't a clue for how long though."

"Well that's just great, it's not like I can just zip off quickly now is it?"

"You know, if you calmed down, slowed down, and found a kinder way to hold a conversation you'd be better off for it."

"Calm down? Slow down? Sir I'll have you know I couldn't get much slower and that sir is the core of my life and problems to date. I'd calm down if I could speed up I can tell you that!"

"I empathize with you. What is your name my fine slow confounded friend?"

"Bill. My name is Bill. It's the quickest name my mother could conjure."

"I tell you what Bill, allow me to conduct a lookout for your safety so that you can do what you are needing to do in cover. What are you needing to do anyway?"

"I need to move me to the end of this branch nearer the trunk. I can smell the greening bark from here."

"Take your time, I'm on lunch digesting."

"I have no choice but to take my time. Thank you for the shelter, once I've made the progress to where I need to be I'll be quite safe." He began to turn his body by changing the direction of his facing face, his shell slowly turned along leaving Jack to witness his very first snail tail.

Bill's tail left a trail of sheen as he progressed up the leaf, onto the very end of the branch and rotated a few degrees to the left to beeline a sheening tail smeared tail trail. His progress was faster than Jack had anticipated.

"Have a lovely day Bill!"

"You as well Crow, I do thank you again." Jack noticed how Bill's shell greened a bit in the shade, how it's color changed just a bit in the darker armpit of the branch where it met the trunk. Bill became part of the tree visually.

With all the bugs, grubs and ants hidden in the pealing bark of the punk trees next to the crepe, a woodpecker wouldn't bother to try to find his friend. It would be a waste of foraging time. Jack looked out again into the sky both for his friend Bill's benefit and his own. It was proving to be a very good day.

*****

Jill perched in the tree behind the bench. The spectacle before her lay out in full obnoxious display. A roller coaster, cranking clacking cars hitched together as a train she'd seen long ago. There were two of them on this roller coaster abomination. While one took on humans, the other ran along the track far up and away. It dipped and dived running faster while the humans screamed louder. Some held on to each other while others raised their arms out into the air screaming louder as well. Some humans shut their eyes, their bodies contorted in dread. Others wore possessed faces expressing crazed ideas to come. Those that filled the still train of cars looked up and over to see those already riding the rails of terror at break neck speeds.

After seating, they pulled a heavy looking collar of bars over their heads and looked at each other laughing with fear or maybe, insanity. Whatever it was it all made no sense whatsoever to Jill. Humans pretending to fly in careening inverted cars. That's what she saw. She heard their voices and realized they didn't come for the exhilaration so much as to be scared out of their minds. Well, good luck with that. They really weren't that smart.

Stiltz was on the ground a tree's root system away foraging for snails and other things. "Do you see him Jill?"

He barely lifted his head to look her way. His interest leaned toward what he could discover below the grass. Sticking your beak where you can't see seemed dicey to Jill's way of thinking. Stiltz did it without a second thought, driving his slopping long beak as deep as he could into the soil. Occasionally he brought up his prized grub worm. There was a method to his madness, which required just a little confidence laced with faith.

"No, no I don't see or hear him anywhere Stiltz, but from the looks of all these people eating all this food I can see why he comes here. This isn't challenging foraging."

"Well, we have to remember who's place this is, Jerry doesn't chose hard anything."

Jill laughed inside her own head. Truer words had never been spoken about Jerry. Easy outs were his choice. Things got hard while trying to find a human to train, so he quit. Which nullified the need to find a girl crow. Which extracted the drive to create a family, which left a bachelor crow out in the world trying to find something better to do that was also easier. That was Jerry. In a nutshell. Which landed on the pavement below her.

Jill looked to the little girl who had thrown it over. "There you are little birdie bird! It's a peanut! Here." The little girl in yellow shorts and a bright white shirt tossed another peanut in the same location. Jill paused.

She'd never met this human before. Why, without payment or training, was this little human offering her food? This was new. This was slightly awkward to a crow to know.

"Aw! Com'on down! I won't bother you. You can have it and I won't even try to pet you little birdiebird." To prove her point the little girl scooted a bit further away from the peanuts, to give Jill a comfortable space. The little girl opened her own peanut to eat and popped the nut into her mouth and dropped the shell on the ground. She smiled up at Jill.
If a girl can't trust another girl, what's this world come to? Jill hopped off her branch and spiraled down to the pavement landing between the two peanuts. They were large. They smelled fresh. They were for her. Jill looked up at the little girl and crowed a thanks.

"You're welcome little birdiebird!" She popped more peanuts in her mouth smiling and chewing at the same time. Jill grabbed one peanut by the claw and speared the second to return to the tree above and eat. It was a bit clumsy going, she probably should have left the one peanut on the ground. This being her first untrained human encounter she wasn't sure that would have been the proper choice. With both claws holding large peanuts she worked on the peanut under her left claw, she was right clawed after all. The little girl watched her eat, their smiles mirrored each other a moment, and then Jill heard a voice call. "Sarah! Let's go honey!"

With that the little girl waved at Jill, giggled and ran towards a waiting mom. They took each other's hands and walked off toward somewhere. Sarah clutched her bag of peanuts in her free hand and swung it forward and back while she skipped along her mother's side.

Jill let go the first peanut shell and started working on the second under her right claw. This place with precise rhinoceros and untrained trained little girls was proving enticing. She found herself happy not to be home at that very moment. What a strange feeling for a very good crow to know.

*****

"That's not the point though!" Jerry tossed back another red worm, feet in soft soils and looking up into the mangroves blocking the sun's demands. His company, a marsh hen, was not interested in his logic. So much so she refused to agree on any points at all! What turned into a friendly chat about grub worms verses red worms, he'd found himself defending the simple statement that he had a right to any opinion at all. Flummoxed again by a marsh hen. He normally avoided them. They were tedious.

"Blah blah blah, Jerry. We've been over this a few times now. I live in a marsh. Therefore you're opinion is moot."

"MOOT! Moot! Amanda when did you become the moot decider? I can have an opinion on worms. I CAN have an opinion on worms if I want!"

"As long as you keep them to yourself."

"The worms or my opinion?"

Amanda was unmoved and unimpressed with his humor. She stepped forward continuing the hunt for the tell tale signs of worms in muck. A small trembling on the surface followed by a bulge attempting to escape her swift beak of wrathful eating.

"Seriously? What's the point of me having an opinion if I can't give it to someone?"

"And there's MY point Jerry. No one around here wants it, so why do you think you need one. You don't. Does your opinion of worms affect my enjoyment of them? No. Does your opinion of worms affect their availability to me? No.

Jerry, does your opinion on worms affect any breathing marsh hen within a day's flight at all? No. And yet you stand there eating them thinking you or I need to hear any of these rambling worm opinion thoughts knocking about in that head of yours. It's as if the conversation last year didn't even happen!"

She went about her business lifting and lowering her bright lime green legs, toes spread wide on each foot allowing her to pad herself across the plants and soils without sinking. Unlike her conversation partner who was forced to keep moving at a pace or seep into the abyss.

"Conversation last year!? Amanda I don't remember what conversation last year. What's that got to do with now?"

"Absolutely nothing. But it does remind me of the time you thought your opinion of the rain held as much affect as the weather itself. It did not. Your opinion of anything is none of my business."

Jerry located a grub fighting it's way to drier ground. He helped it on it's way by swallowing it whole.

"Amanda, your opinion of my opinion is none of my business."

"Ah! And so another crow wakes up to his own truths." She disappeared behind a curtain of under brush, a soft airy laugh hanging in the humid air.

Jerry stood too still too long to ponder Amanda's last words. He was knee high in muck. But he felt a red worm stir under his left claw. All things being equal, his opinion held.

*****

The art of bonsai allows the nurturing artist to create visual suggestions of other places, otherscapes. A tree can grow as a waterfall, a mountain range, billowing clouds, or scraping winds on a mountainside. A tree is a canvas open to interpretation and manipulation.

Lisa viewed the hundreds of trees within her vision to be a personal bonsai forest. Her favorite was the pine tree directly in her view. It begged for a nurturing artist's pruning. At 50 feet it would most likely disagree. Her eyes wondered to the top branches hoping to catch a glimpse of Jack. He'd been gone a long time. With his absence came the absences of Twigg, Barbosa, and Edgar as well. Her crows had vanished into the seasons.

Butters weighed a little over two pounds and Lisa felt every ounce of that on her shoulder. A macaw tongue inserted itself into her ear. This was Butters making sure Lisa noticed her company. Lisa loved her parrots. She loved Butters for being a big butterball of opposites. Hold me. Don't touch me. Love me. Go away. Somewhere in her family ancestry was a cat and a one night stand.

Her gaze followed the lines of the trees as quietly has her right hand ran the length of Butters tail feathers. Measured gently along the way. She cast a wish out into the universe for her crows to return, and then turned into the house to set Butters back on her cage door. She should eat some lunch. Lazy girl.

Lisa walked through the bird room, through the half bath, left into the hallway right through the dining room, pausing to say hello to her rabbit and give both her guinea pigs an ear rub.

Werthers and Basil needed baths. She set that calendar item in her head for the weekend. Lisa loved her furry little ones. She paused to look out the dining room window to see who was in the front yard. The usual cast of characters. Her ducks, a few squirrels and three ibis for good measure. She grabbed the yellow bowl filled with leftover and rejected parrot foods and opened the door to the front yard. Lunch for her ducks. They scrambled to meet her and hiss their approvals. Lisa loved her ducks.

She tossed lunch far and wide so that there would be no arguments about access and availability to items. She closed the door behind listening to duck chatter and hisses. Muscovy ducks vocalized like no duck she knew growing up in Illinois. Her ducks were hilarious. Opinionated. Pushy. Confident. Her ducks were her obsession. Such an obsession in a State that has an over abundance of them can cause conversations not planned.

Recently her husband answered the front door because Lisa was busy reading a book ignoring her phone and door knockers. He said hello, and disappeared outside closing the door behind. A few minutes passed and he opened the door yelling, "Honey, can you come out here?"

"Sure!" Sure in their house was looking every parrot and one hound in the eye reminding them she could see through walls and hear everything. "Be good."

She opened the door to find her husband and a tall uniformed Florida Wildlife Officer. He was backed up against the house, surrounded by begging ducks. Lisa felt bad for him, he couldn't shoot his way out of this situation.

Lisa offered the wife to husband look "Well this is interesting." He responded with the husband to wife look, "You knew this was going to happen sooner or later."

Lisa looked up and gave the Officer her full attention. And shook his hand. She liked wildlife police. Also, she knew her rights. So they were on the same page.

"Ma'am we received a report of your feeding wildlife, specifically Muscovy ducks. The caller is concerned that they may get run over crossing the street due to the feedings."

"Oh, I see. Well they cross the street because their foraging path has always started by leaving the lake. They just added us to their natural route."

"I see."

Melinda Muscovy was pressing his personal space. The Officer glanced down at the duck pressing his personal space. Lisa waited for her to start pulling on his shoelaces. She's not a patient girl.

"Well it's my job to let you know what the law states."

She smiled big. She knew her rights. "Oh yes! I've read the statutes."

"Oh. That's excellent. Well you know that you can feed these ducks."

"Yes."

"You know that you can not feed protected species. Of which I don't see any here among these ducks."

Leon joined Melinda in the press. This Officer was back against the wall with his hand rested on his weapon. He hadn't unsnapped the holster, yet. He must be used to the pressure of a dozen ducks not caring one bit about laws or statutes.

Melinda looked up at Lisa. "What's with this guy?"

Lisa shrugged back in her direction letting her know it wasn't anything to worry about. But they better discuss it later. Best to press on. Melinda said something under her breath to Leon her mate. Most likely smart ass and unhelpful.

Lisa smiled again. "So if a protected species were to join the ducks, I would have to stop. Considering that law."

"Yes ma'am. But I only see you have these ducks, there's really nothing to worry about."

"Yes, I know." She smiled. Again.

Her husband stood behind me. Her rock. Her power source. Her patient loving spouse patiently witnessing the law meeting a law abiding citizen knowing her laws and rights. He also knows these ducks are on their last nerve. Three humans and not one yellow bowl of anything tossed. They were an insult to the B&B industry. These barbarians could storm the gates at any minute. This guy could loose his military specific shoelaces and there would be nothing she could do about it.

"I do have to tell you that anyone can, with written consent, trap and humanely euthanized these ducks."

"Yes. I am aware."

"Well, my work here is done then. I thank you for your time. I'll file a report saying we've closed this investigation."

It was then she saw a fully trained professional in bullet proof clothing, mil spec boots, loaded weapon, and full radio capabilities try to decide whether he would step over a dozen ducks, or shuffle through the horde demanding recompense for the disruption of services.

Before he left Lisa shook his hand. The good shake learned long ago at a business weekend training seminar. You shake with the dominate hand, and cup the joined hands underneath with your other hand. Then you look directly into the eyes of a professional you both admire and appreciate and you tell them your most sincere thank you. And she did. Lisa told him she appreciated what he and his colleagues do every day. And that she appreciated his visit to clarify the current goings on around their property. She was far too happy and excited for him. Now he really wanted to leave.

Melinda wanted fed.

As he walked the 30 feet of front porch out to his vehicle Leon, Tony, Morty, and the new guy Lisa hadn't named yet, slowly followed him out. Walking their best badass boy duck struts. To make sure he left without any trouble. Because they could make that trouble for this guy. If he pushed it. The girls looked at Lisa. Lisa looked at her husband.

"I wonder who called?" They had their guesses on that matter. But, it didn't matter.

For the inconvenience of it all Lisa fed the flock extra bonus rounds. Parrot pellets and all the good stuff she saved for breakfast service. Lisa refreshed their always fresh water bowl. She smiled. Again.

Her husband once said she couldn't name every wild thing that showed up in the yard. Lisa took this as a challenge.

Yes she could, and she would also refer to them as hers. Because what does a human like most but to take ownership of things wild, companion, or saved from the evil world of nature. She'd seen what nature can do if an osprey had intentions.

She sat on the couch with Angus. Sixty nine and half pounds of Catahoula hound devoted to her and her baked sweet potatoes. Her eyes wandered to the windows with no crows on the other side. She knew they weren't really hers. She knew the ducks weren't hers. The possum that came out at around 5:30 every afternoon, he wasn't hers either. What she owned was the adoration, awe, and love for them all. What a marvel each and every personality. She named them as an act of kinship. She'd prefer a wild thing's company to most humans. You couldn't know for a truth why a human chose your company. But when a wild thing looks you in the eye quietly ordering you to feed it. There was a unspeakable bond of slavery. Her ducks had names she gave them because they were her beloved bosses willing to accept her and order her around.

Lately as the hurricanes became Godzilla like, and the temperatures rose to stupid degrees, and the waters grew hot becoming brewing bacteria petri dishes she and her husband toyed with moving a bit North. Not North as in winter comes here, but North as in a winter that isn't that bad and won't require ski gear comes here. Tennessee. Southern Tennessee. But it fell to who would care for all her ducks? Her ducks. They would be lost without her. Which is why she took a deep breath even thinking of abandoning them to some decrepit animal ignorer who would buy their house and turn it into an anti-animal fortress of hate.

Who would rescue turtles stuck at the fence line unable to think around a corner to continue on to the lake? She taxied a dozen turtles a season from the back yard fence line through the house and out to the front yard. Pausing to show the parrots her charge. Butters was never impressed. Snickers screamed hello.

She would carefully set them down pointing their nose in a perfect straight line directed squarely at the perfect opening under the neighbor's fence that led to the lake. They didn't need to think, just scuttle. She couldn't abandon her turtles. She still felt an ache for Tortellini who hatched too early in the cold season last year. Tortellini was found by her husband while he fixed a sprinkler head. He brought it in the house for immediate emergency sMothering.

Tortellini spent the cold spell in a turtle tank Lisa quickly set up that day. Because if you live near a lake and a tidal creek you had to have a turtle tank, clean and ready. He grew fast with hand feedings and bedtime stories. She took him across the street and released him into the lake. Tossing in all his remaining krill food after him. Out of depths of the waters came a battalion of tilapia of all sizes. Drawn to a delicacy not had often. They devoured Tortellini's packed lunch in minutes. Leaving him with only the lake to sustain him. She wondered if he'd suffered an awful lonely death without her. Angus stretched out long with a hound force uninterested in sharing the couch with the human currently in the way.

Angus was definitely hers. He took great lengths to express this to her every day and night. Draping across the back of the couch, resting his hind quarters on her shoulder, beating her in the face with a long happy flapping tail. Watching her every move to make sure she didn't carelessly wander off into some dark forest, thereby getting lost.

During the day while playing out in the back yard he runs full force at the back door slamming hound feet hard to knock and get her attention. A toy hanging from his mouth. He would stand four feet in the window looking for her to acknowledge the invitation to throw it for him, so that he could catch it and keep it away from her. Always a game that said I am yours, this is mine. Angus needed something to need him, too.
We all need feeling needed.

*****

Butters jumped off Lisa's shoulder to land on her favorite spot. Her spot gave a full view through windows to the deck outside. It also gave her full view to the tall tree behind her house to keep an eye out of annoying things. It also gave her full view out the same windows to keep an eye on the ground and all the turtles that may crawl out of Tinney Creek. Turtles with no common sense or self respect. Butters hated turtles.

"You need to calm down." Snickers perched on his favorite spot. In the center of a room full of windows looking out onto everything and then some. Depending on how you turned your head. Being a parrot, he could turn his head anywhere and how he wanted. He sat at the top of the tall tree at the center of the room with all the windows to keep an eye on everything. Because male scarlet macaws were made for this job. Keeping an eye on everything.

"I am calm." Butters spoke into the window, but over her shoulder. She didn't need to give Snickers the look. Snickers knew quite well he said stupid things.

"If you were calm, you'd stop staring out that window. You aren't calm. You're stalking trouble. I know it. You know it. Even Felix knows it."

Felix perched in front of his particular window from his particularly favorite spot keeping an eye on the neighbor who had proven himself insane. Nothing he did made sense.

"Don't drag me into your macaw mess. Neither one of you are calm. You are both landmines waiting for something to trigger you. You are a constant threat. And annoying." Felix did not bother to turn around to deliver the verdict of an African Grey with better things to do than discuss truths with two macaws. He had an insane neighbor to keep an eye on.

"You're both interrupting my concentration. If I miss anything and we all die because of a turtle that made its way into the house, that's on you." Butters settled deeper into her perch.

"You need to calm down."

"You said that already."

"You haven't acknowledged I'm right."

"Well, you're right about that part."

Felix climbed off his tree stand in front of his window. The insane neighbor walked back into the house. He could take a break. Monkey like without the assist of a tail, Felix smoothly ascended the bars of his open cage to place himself in front of his play stand top with a bowl of his favorite breakfast snacks. One does not take chances with the low blood sugar threat while under threat of insane neighbors. He grabbed a dry pasta wheel and cracked the outer edge to make his way to the cog. "If you two spent as much time trying not to be annoying as you do trying to have a conversation, I wouldn't have to keep an eye on you! I only have two eyes. Do you want the insane neighbor to find his way in here? I think not." He snapped another section of wheel exposing more cog.

"Whatever. You've been over there for 7 years and I personally have not seen this insane human you go on about daily. I can see out your window, I only see some guy carrying a shovel. Or a hose. Once he threw a ball for his dog to chase. I've never seen your insane human yet. You need to calm down." Snickers tipped his head waiting for an answer to a finely tuned accusation.

Felix snapped a third section wheel and tossed it on the floor. He wanted the cog. It tasted better. "Maybe you don't understand the threat here. Maybe you are so busy trying to be a tough guy you are no longer a thinking guy. Maybe without me here you'd already be dead. I can't calm down, we'll all die!"

Butters stretched her left wing with the help of her left leg and foot. You can't stretch a wing without a leg and foot. The best stretch ends with a talon fist clenching into a perfect talon ball. She turned around to deliver "the look". Felix paid no attention just as he had done before breakfast. She tossed a look of "exhaustion" at Snickers. He stuffed his head into his food bowl. How can a girl make a point if no one pays attention!?

The room settled into a quiet hum of an air conditioner kicking on, and an Indian ring neck hurling 156 grams of himself through a quieted room at the speed of Kirby. He landed on Butters' cage with a furious thump creating a large dollop of angst inside Butters' brain. She called out a sharp rebuke to his disturbance of her world and thoughts.

"GAH! What is your problem Kirby? Why can't you land like an average parrot? I hate that thud."

"I am above average. I will land with an above average focus."
He wiped his beak on the cage rail rapidly. Claiming
ownership of the space and cleaning off the warm sweet
potatoes he'd just eaten. "What's the problem anyway, you're
just napping."

"Napping? NAPPING!? I am keeping an eye on things.
Clearly."

"I'm pretty sure that's napping. Felix is napping. Snickers is
napping. You're all napping."

Felix, Snickers and Butters pulled their heads up straight,
pinning parrot pupils in indignation, they shouted in three
separate voices creating a chorus of offended individuals.
"NO WE ARE NOT! You almost died and you don't even
know it!"

Lisa entered the room to triage why all her parrots were
screaming. She'd hoped it would be her crows on the deck
causing the cacophony. It could be a turtle, or the neighbor or
a vulture outside though. The possibilities were endless with
these four.

She turned the corner to see everyone in their place. Kirby was
laughing, the rest were screaming. Kirby's laugh resembled a
buzzy radio while you turned the dial to find the clear radio
signal. He laughed. Butters, Snickers and Felix did not.

"Alright what's going on in here?" Lisa looked out the deck.
No crows had come. She looked out the windows. No turtles.
No neighbor. No vultures in the tree hunting dead things.
"Well, we're not under attack so what's your problem?"

They all had an answer in their own voice and way. She stood in front of Snickers to let him tell her his frustrations in his Mugwai. "Poor Snickers. He suffers so, huh buddy?" She handed him a almond.

Butters stopped complaining and waited for hers. Lisa ran the palm of her hand over Butters' head lightly feeling her feathers fall back against her head gently. "Butterbean you shouldn't let the boys bug you. You know you're the smartest in here." Butters purred and accepted two almonds. Because being outnumbered required more treats.

Felix scrambled to his tree stand to wait for his conversation. He didn't want the almond. He wanted to be heard. He wanted his time in court and to be heard.

Lisa approached with a smile. Felix wasn't going to let her pet him, that's not how Felix works. He wanted to speak his mind and to make sure she knew his basic parrot rights were being infringed upon.

"Okay, Fee. Tell me all about your suffering at the wings of others. Who's fault is it today? Hmmm…"

"Yapplepopcorn! BAD BIRD. See the birdie? BAD BIRD! Pfft!" Lisa followed his eyes that pointed all the blame on Kirby. She looked back to Felix. Basically Kirby was being Kirby which on a good day is annoying. "I totally get it Felix. He's a blue menace!" Felix appreciated elevated verbal drama with his pity.

Animals appreciated understanding, just like humans. The difference being animals knew exactly what they needed to be understood about.

Humans not so much. Her fellow beings tended to rationalize, self edit and self write truths to support habits and systems that supported their own world. Their own world being anything they could touch. You could attempt to tell someone else you understood them. You could do your level best to stand alongside them in empathy. But it was always a moving target. Depending on what new information someone else told them about their world that touched them and only those they agreed with at any given moment.

Human's didn't want understanding, they wanted attention that said they were right.

Inside her experiences parrots, and crows now, wanted to be understood on the levels of need. Needs to be part of a group where all members were equal and important. Flocking is important. Security and food. Or better yet, food security. Knowing where to go and when to go there to get what you needed to eat. Her ducks appreciated that and were quick to wag their big duck tails in thanks at every meal served. Her ducks were so confident in her work they lined up outside the dining room window to stare holes through the glass reminding her she understood their food security needs.

Her parrots were content to accept a sloppy unreliable human into their flock. All she had to do was be consistent and sincere. Or better yet, sincerely consistent. That's difficult for a human. They think too much about the things that mean nothing at all.

Her crows needed consistent trades. A crow didn't want handouts, they preferred a good collaboration on matters. And had no problem taking the time to pay it forward with shiny things and odds and ends found through out the day.

She kept her crow payments and offerings in a clay bowl in her office. The stones, shells, buttons, feathers, found flotsam and remnants of human single use reminded her life isn't necessarily fair, but you could be fair inside it.

She missed her crows. She missed Jack. She missed knowing sooner or later she'd hear a call and find a crow waiting with shells lined up at his feet. Lisa looked forward to a good crow trade. She missed looking into the eyes of a transaction of faith.

*****

At this point Jill felt like a spectacle. She stood on the back of what Stiltz explained to be an elephant. The elephant explained his name was Don. Stiltz, Jill and a handful of local ibis stood on the back of a lumbering elephant named Don as he led his herd of elephant family along a path edged with long wild grasses. Within eye shot stood a group of humans waving at them, talking to each other and tossing peanuts into the enclosure. Some peanuts landed on a grassy knoll where elephants could wonder. Most fell short into a moat that made sure no human could get to any elephant.

This entire place seemed to have one goal. Have as many humans in one place that can not in any way shape or form, get to as many animals kept in one place. And there, inside this strange labyrinth of human paths and living areas they all stared at each other and said nothing to each other. This place felt clogged up. This place felt flooded with nonsense and noise and food that didn't support life. It only supported itself so that it could do it over and over and over insincerely.

"Where are we going Don?"

"To the water hole behind the rocks to find shade without humans."

Elephants didn't mince words. They only said what they meant and not one more extra word was added for affect or punctuation. She found herself liking elephants.

"I appreciate you letting me ride along, Don."

"A friend of Stiltz is a friend of mine. Tony! Catch up to your mother! Leave that butterfly alone. He's got places to be." Unminced herd leader instructions fell on the smaller floppy ears of a baby elephant. He startled his attention back to the herd now ahead of him.

Baby elephants giggle most all the time. If they aren't giggling under their breath they are working on figuring out their nose. An elephant nose is a lot to understand. An elephant nose takes years of practice. You can breath with it. Pick things up. Put things down. Grab your mother's tail. Grab a wrong tail. Grab sticks and hit things with the stick you picked up. If you are lucky you can convince a butterfly to sit on it. You can drink water with it. You can spray water with it. You can take baths with it, and throw dust for a dust bath afterwards. The trick to your nose is knowing when to do any of that and when not to do some of it. You can't drink water and breath at the same time, he assumed. He would have to test that idea out at the water hole. The idea sounded right in his head though. He giggled and kicked up his feet a bit to catch up to the herd and his mother.

Jill took in the sight of a mother and child's love on full display. No matter the name, no matter the kind a mother and child's love shown the same. They needed each other to complete themselves.

The ground rumbled above as the unsettled dirt fell from the ceilings of the tunnel he just dug. Hercules shook his head in dismay. Of all the places elephants had to walk, they walked over his place. Hercules, being a rhinoceros beetle, not to be confused with the rigorous rhino named Gregory that lived above ground, found it a struggle to create the perfect place to find a perfect girl. Or for that matter the perfect level of alone. Sometime between now and then the elephant's started walking over his tunneled lands. He would move, but it's the principle of the thing. It's easier for an elephant not to step in a certain area, than it is for a beetle to make all new tunnels in a certain new area. And besides, he was here first!

The rumbling rambles of the elephant herd continued over head. A quicker paced step declared the end of it. The baby elephant didn't lumber like the rest. He skipped over.

Ox beetles didn't ask for much. Because Ox beetles aren't that much in size. They just needed good loose soils, composting natural things that rot, and cover of leaves or long grasses, or both. He'd found this area under the tree close enough to the water to create just the right spot for an ox beetle to flourish. He'd done this seasons ago. He had been here first!

Digging tunnels isn't just digging tunnels for an Ox beetle. It's digging up to make holes out into the world to not only see where every other beetle may be but to make sure air came down into his tunnel system. Rotting things that taste good tend to smell up a tunnel. Tunneling up and out every so often was a good strategy as well when a murderous egret shows up.

A quick beetle, knowing his exits and entrances didn't need to worry about a murderous egret. But if lumbering elephants rumbling loose his ceiling didn't change he would be forced to spend more time creating stronger ceilings than tunnels. Less tunnels means less exits that means less areas to harvest and look for a girl.

Hercules miffed over the situation. He climbed out one of his strategically placed exits to locate the offending elephants. They were at the water hole and would be staying there the day. He could take the time to create more tunnel length toward the tree trunk. Make a nice exit at it's base. And if time permitted take a walk about the tree trunk to see if there were any nice girls. He wasn't getting any younger. He'd be turning 5 months soon and then it was all downhill from there.

*****

"I can almost see the other shore if I look carefully."

This was his 9th visit with Ardon at the shore of the Bay. But the sight still held his imagination. So much living water filled with so many others he'd still not met.

"There's another water that's even bigger than this one, it's on the other side of the land. You have to fly west to get there. It's not far though."

West led home. There was more water on the other side of his life? How could he not know all these things all his life? More, bigger, new. He felt surrounded by questions he didn't know to ask.

"You probably couldn't cross that water like you do this one. It's bigger than you can fly all at once." Ardon kept a distracted look out for anoles and other lizards that might come out of hiding. They made a nice snack.

Jack perched paying no mind to lizards or edible things. He
fancied the thought of traveling west to find this other water.
He could stop and visit his flock on the way. If he told Jill
about what he's found, he might be able to talk her into going
there with him.

"Has Jerry been to the other water Ardon?"

"He's never spoken of it. Knowing our friend Jerry I would
think it not likely. He's easily amused. And there is more than
enough of that on this side of it all." He stabbed quickly at a
movement in the grass. An anole lost. Ardon tossed the limp
body back into his mouth. The tail was uncooperative but he
managed to swallow it whole with a shake of the head and a
wiggle of the neck.

Quinlin screamed in terror at witnessing her beloved Gottfried
sliding down the throat of a dreaded beast. Quinlin ran back
into the depths of the marsh and it's twisted grasses and
mangrove roots. She skittered under a wet rotting leaf to catch
her breath and compartmentalize what just happened.
She slowed her breath. She considered her options. For an
anole there were endless options for traveling and surviving.
An anole could live to a ripe old age of three seasons or so.
The rules were clear though. Stay where you can't be seen.
Hunt where only you can hunt. Sleep where others leave for
the night. Find your own kind, keep your distances. More
than one lizard draws a crowd of beasts.

She'd met Gottfried under a small bush on the other side of
the sandy beach. It was an act of fate since she rarely traveled
across that open sandy beach. A lizard could not run, skitter,
trot, slither, or slitter fast enough for her taste.

That day presented a good enough reason to try it, at dusk. There was a buzzy mass of flies lighting and hovering over something.

These weren't the nasty greenhead flies that argue and laugh at lizards, but sand flies. Greenhead flies would bite back just as much as laugh at you for trying to eat them. Sand flies were too busy eating rotting kelp and trying to lay sand fly eggs. They didn't bite back, either. Seeing a cloud of inviting sand flies was just enough to convince Quinlin to run over the large swatch of sandy beach to the high tide line offering flotsam, and shed grasses and kelp from the depths. A perfect place to find other tasty bits that were too busy to notice her. She was the same color as the dead kelp as well. That coincidence created successful hunts.

As the sun sat on the horizon resting before it's last setting she skittered quickly to take advantage of a handful of minutes to dine quietly on sand flies. She ran right into Gottfried who was headed in the opposite direction. There was no shadow to judge distances by and they both were wrong about the others location. She bounced off his head, or maybe he off hers, either perspective ended in a heap facing each other.

"Well, that didn't work out at all, did it!" Gottfried laughed and rubbed his head with his hand.

"I think we misjudged just about everything that mattered." Quinlin laughed along shaking her head to realign her thoughts.

"Where are you going? I'm Gottfried and I was heading over there to that tall grass by the water."

"I'm Quinlin. I just left that place. There's nothing to eat there, I ate the only cricket. I'm going to that cloud of sand flies hovering over the kelp." She pointed with her tail, it was easier to keep her scuttled balance.

"Oh, those are greenhead flies. I wouldn't recommend going over there. They're in some sort of argument about who gets to harass the two humans wrapped up in a towel under a bush not far away."

"That's silly. There's plenty of human for that many greenhead flies. I bet they could double their number and still have skin space leftover to bite."

"RIGHT! That's what I told them straight to their faces. Ingrates."

"Well, if there's nothing there, or over there and we're here. I suppose it's best to call it a day."

"I suppose if you think on it Quinlin, we were just meant to find a friend today. I'm glad I ran into you."

"I'm glad you ran into me too, Gottfried."

*****

Ardon lifted himself back to the middle branches of the mangrove bush. It was a wing flap effort that stationed him next to Jack. Time for a nap. Jack was gazing out into the water, he looked agreeable to a nap. Ardon adjusted his feathers, then wings and one foot up.

"I think I might just fly over to this other water. Maybe stop at my flock's trees and visit my family on the way. I have a friend named Jill, maybe she'd be interested in seeing the bigger water. If I tell her about you and all the things on this side." Jack closed his eyes to fall into an afternoon rest.

"I met Jill. She seems nice." Ardon used his last bit of awake to speak.

Jack shot out of his nap shifting with a jolt. "You met Jill!?" He reeled from the thought of it. She was here? She flew here? Surely Ardon didn't go there. How did she get here? Did Jerry bring her? The questions erupted in his mind, but not one left his mouth.

Ardon heard Jack's questions in the silence that lived between them. "Stiltz brought her. She asked Stiltz to find you. But you don't keep too many habits so all I could tell them was you were here at our last visit, and that maybe you were at the park, or with Jerry."

Jack's stomach dropped. Well there it is. The thorn in all of this free wheeling adventure business. No one that's important really knows where you are, and you don't know where they are either. He perched in this empty space alone. He had no idea where Jill was now. And she didn't know where he was, and this was a much bigger world than the one they both left. They could go on missing each other for seasons.

Ardon could feel the tension through the branch they shared. "Jack they were heading to see Gregory. She could be there. Or maybe with Don. Either one will get you into the general vicinity."

The one emotion felt throughout all living beings on earth is loss. How loss is interpreted and handled between the species reveals the species. If a creature misses a food, another of it's kind, or a seasonal requirement they go about finding it. Creating it. Replaying it. Completing it. Creatures just do the things that need doing until something bigger eats them.

Humans call this instinct. Humans put ideas in boxes alphabetically stacked, listed, and saved. This creates a convenient way to retrieve things they intend on avoiding. Because control is camouflage for responsibility. Humans sit in groups holding devices redefining their losses. They herd according to their devices and what they choose to look at on those devices. The only mammal walking on two legs walks in circles, rationalizing to avoid handling situations such as loss, loneliness or fear. Or what to make for dinner. These devices provide group think. A convenient way to avoid that tedium known as a "real conversation" with a real human. They can't be trusted. Particularly with dinner plans.

Some creatures would call this instinct. Still others would call it the problem. This is neither here nor there for a crow. Jack, being crow, took flight without fanfare. Ardon grinned. There went a crow that didn't know the why or the how. He was just doing what he felt right. A fine crow. Ardon slipped into his nap knowing he would never see Jack Crow again. Jack had things to accomplish that would take a lifetime.

*****

"You've been here all your life?"

"Yes. The whole time up to this very minute."

Jerry grabbed another red worm from the pile of worms he and toad shared under the heavy leaves of a fern. The shade was cool, the ground moist and the worms easy pickings.

"So you've never once left to toad somewhere else?"

"Where exactly would I go for better toading?"

"I don't know. I'm not a toad. But there may be some other toadier toading place. Aren't you worried you're missing all that toadiness?"

"Are you mocking me?"

When Jerry first invited him to lunch he'd reluctantly agreed. Only because he knew Jerry had no interest in eating him for lunch and because if he had lunch with Jerry there would be larger share of worms. Jerry was very good at catching red worms. A marsh hen had given him some pointers some where along his travels. His reluctance grew from having had lunch with Jerry before. Inevitably the bird just couldn't stay away from asking questions about why he toaded in one area, rather than traveling about to toad in new places.

They'd been over this before, a number of times. The first attempt at the subject led to an afternoon debate about the amount of work it requires to jump to someplace rather than fly. Jerry was adamant that flying was just as hard as jumping. Easy for him to say.

The second lunch debate entailed the stupidity of leaving a perfectly good woody place that offered everything a toad would need without having to wonder.

The third lunch debate added the points that toads do not wander. Toads do not wonder why they don't wander. And the oldest toad known to toads lived that long precisely because he did not wonder.

And here they ate, under the same heavy leaf fern chewing on worms and the same subject, again. This had to be mockery at this point. Because there was no point. In fact, it was none of Jerry's business why he did or did not do anything or nothing. Where did this crow get off anyway?

"I'm not mocking you Durden. I'm just curious. Call it lunch curious."

"Ha! You're judgmental and nosey that's what you are Jerry. You compare me with you and don't even bother to understand me first. Or Last."

They sat in front of their squirming worm pile eating in silence. Jerry hadn't a clue why Durden didn't have an answer, but he was coming to the conclusion that no other creature had an answer to this question either. They all had reasons why they stayed in their place. They all gave clear concise reasons why they didn't need to wander at all. Jerry looked down to see one remaining worm.

"You eat it Durden. I'm full."

"Yes, you are full of your self. And I don't mind if I do." He toadily snatched the last worm with his long spring loaded sticky tipped instrument of death dealing. Durden preferred calling his tongue a death dealing instrument. It sounded impressive.

"Thanks for lunch Durden, I'm on my way to find a friend."

"You have friends?" Durden laughed out loud while embedding himself into the soil with digging back legs. He flung soil and leaf until his body was perfectly backed into a toady hole. He used those same feet to flip loose soil and leafs over his back and neck until only two toad nostrils and two toad eyes were above ground. Why would he leave this perfect place for some place that may, or may not, be real at all? Ridiculous crow conversations were exhausting. But the worm count helped.

*****

Jill perched in the shading tree above the zebra. Stiltz had left her to do his own foraging. Zed kept her company while she waited for Jerry. What were the odds a turtle could predict the future, or a Jerry's next move. In either event allowing him to vent his troubles for a few hours paid off. She would join Jerry to find Jack and finally know all was well for all, although slightly scattered.

"You crows are quite varied. Have you noticed this fact?" Zed didn't bother to look up to Jill's location. He continued grass foraging ripping up a large cluster of peanut grass that did not taste at all like peanuts. Humans and their naming word mash.

"I would think we are as varied as any creature, including a zebra. Maybe you've just not met enough crow to know."

"Good point. You are the third I've bothered to chat with for any length of time. How many members are in your flock?"

"373, but our family flock is 37 of that. And to be honest, I probably only talk to 7 of those."

Zed ripped more peanut grass and looked up at a very honest crow. How specific she tended to answer his questions. She left little to the imagination for later stories he could tell his herd behind the boulders. If he tried to use this information to create a crow tale it would end up sounding like gossip. He did not gossip. He shared stories. He would need more answers with less information if he was going to leave this Jill with a good story to tell later.

Zed appreciated Jerry for being able to deliver answers without information. The stories that bird provided were priceless! His whole 'I ate a dead turtle egg' story had the girl zebras screaming 'EW!' And the boy zebras laughing their stripes off. It's still a story they ask for at the water hole.

"Do you eat dead turtle eggs Jill?"

"Do I look like Jerry?"

"Oddly, yes, but I suppose that's the burden of your species." Jill had a response but Jerry's arrival interrupted thoughts and minds.

"Jill! Wow! You're here, I'm here, Jack's somewhere here. I would not have bet on this if I was betting! Hey Zed!"

"Jerry."

Jerry perched in the tree near Jill's branch. She looked good. She hadn't changed a bit. "So did Stiltz show you around?"

"Yes. He's given me quite a tour. Where's Jack?" She'd had enough of small talking. She'd done it since arriving on this side of the world.

"He's somewhere."

"How none specific of you."

"Well, he knows where we are so I suppose he's on his way. I sent word through the Petra and Setra. We just need to sit tight and let him hear about us. Petra and Setra never fail to get the word out."

*****

Jack perched on the middle boulder of Gregory's boulder collection. He'd just have to rest here to start his hunt again. He'd not found Jill anywhere on this side of the roller coaster. He could have easily missed her, or be ahead of her flight pattern. This was maddening. He hopped to the outer boulder, it's height giving him a better view of the sky's traffic.

"Gregory isn't here."

Jack continued his sky scanning, "Yes. I know Henry. I'm just here for a rest. Your boulder is the best place to keep an eye on the sky."

"I wouldn't know anything about that, but it does seem to bring in flyers. What are you keeping an eye out about?" Henry crawled out from under his duo boulder fortress and shook the dust from his tail. He'd need to dig that opening a bit wider. Or stop eating at the roller coaster. Jack looked a bit jumpy today. He scurried around and further away from his boulders to get a better view up. "So what are you looking for Jack?"

He squinted into the sun. He saw nothing but more sun. "A friend. She's traveling with Stiltz Ibis. I don't know if you know him. Or her for that matter, but I'm looking for her specifically."

"I know Stiltz. He's presumptuous."

Henry had met Stiltz a season or two ago. He was minding his own business under his boulder fortress. He was taking a nap to rest for the remaining day's work of squirreling away for the winter months. He was rudely awakened by a probing beak from above. What a presumptuous ibis.

Henry knew plenty of ibis thanks to Gregory. They flew in numbers to land on him or the ground and eat the bugs he kicked up or carried on his hide. Gregory said he appreciated their work, and didn't mind them tagging along. He couldn't reach the middle of his back to scratch off the annoying insects.

Henry had become comfortable with waking up during the day to crawl out of his boulder fortress and find dozens of meandering ibis slowly foraging and walking back and forth in no particular order or fashion. They honked softly. They hardly made any noise at all. They kept to their business and their side of the grass and boulders. And they didn't waste time with small talk. Which any ground squirrel can appreciate in the fall. There's squirreling to do.

But the morning Stiltz showed up his opinion changed. In the dark he saw a small fissure open in the soil letting in the light, he saw a yellow beak descend and poke him directly in the belly. He felt the poke. He saw the beak ascend and disappear leaving the slightest slash of light still visible. A wound in the ground where his privacy leaked out. How rude! Who would do such a thing?

The beak reappeared a few inches away from his head. Henry had to dodge a rude beak driving into his den. How utterly vile!

He scrambled up and out of his fortress to find Stiltz, bending at the knee reaching as far as he could under the boulders to drive his rude, obnoxious beak deep into his burrow. "Do you mind!"

"No."

"Do you know you are piercing the very center of my home and den with your filthy face?"

"My face isn't filthy and it's not my face piercing anything. It's my beak. But my apologies. I'll move to another area. Unless you've squirreled away snails, grubs, or worms in there."

"Snails, grubs, or WORMS!? Who do you think I am?"

"I wouldn't presume."

"HA! Wouldn't presume, as you presumptuously pierce my den! Who are you anyway? So that I can remember the name of the rudest ibis I have ever been forced to meet."

"Stiltz. My name is Stiltz and I personally know another ibis that's way more rude than me. You'd hate him."

"Rude and inappropriate! Here you stand talking behind the back of a friend. I am not surprised. You are derelict."

"I'm not talking behind his back. He's right behind you following me."

Henry spun on his paws ending his turn looking directly at a beak embedded in the ground just inches away. He looked into the eyes of another rude ibis. Where do they all come from?

"I'm sure you have someplace to be that's not in front of me, squirrel."

Shocked and annoyed. He would not admit Stiltz was right about his friend. He would not!

"As a matter of needs at the moment yes, I do."

Ibis were just fine on top of a rhino. The minute you let them wander around the place they get lippy. He asked Gregory to keep an eye out for more boulders that could be rolled near his boulder fortress thereby enlarging the protected area. Which in turn would keep a rude ibis at bay. To date, no extra boulders had been found. A pity.

Jack hopped down to the ground grabbing Henry's attention with the winds escaping his wings. "Sorry to hear you find Stiltz presumptuous. I suppose an ibis can be that way under the right circumstances. Have you seen him lately?"

"No, I have not. When he does arrive he rides in on Gregory though. Who's the other friend he's with? Another presumptuous ibis?"

"No. She's a crow. Her name is Jill. We've been friends since hatching."

"Humph. Well, I'll certainly keep an eye out and let her know I know you. You might want to try the zebras, too. They're so close. And you know Zed. He'll be quick about helping you. And precise."

"I'll do that. If Jerry, Jill, or Stiltz show up, let them know I'm at Zed's okay?"

"I will do that. I can't say I'll enjoy telling Mr. Presumptuous."

Jack laughed at that last comment. Only because he's heard that before, but in reference to Jerry. He flew due south toward the zebra plain. They were scattered under and around their favored trees enjoying shade and dust bathing. Jack appreciated a good dust bath himself. At the very least he could let Zed know he was looking for his friends and take a dust bath before the sun started it's descent.

*****

"I kid you not there are zebra like you that don't have stripes! Not one stripe!" Jerry and Jill stood in the shorter grass looking up into the faces of zebra foraging the grasses. The conversation had turned from the excellence of being a zebra to the idea that there were zebra with no stripes. None of them accepted Jerry's hypothesis.

"And if we were to believe your little story of stripe less zebra, what do they call themselves? And I am not saying we believe a word you are saying." Garland ripped more grass from the ground and turned to look at Hamer with a nod of agreement. They weren't falling for another of Jerry Crow's personal jokes.

Jill shifted her stance in the grass. She looked upwards seeking relief from three males arguing about things that have no affect on their current situation. What was it with men and needing to be right about things that don't matter rather than right about what matters. She glanced at the zebra who had lined up in zebra head row of 5 waiting for Jerry to support his claim with facts he could easily make up anyway.

This was ludicrous. This was her life. What was she doing here anyway? She had plenty of goals and items to attend to at home. What matter was it that Jerry dragged Jack off into the unknown for some adventure?

What started all this anyway? Now she stood between defiant zebras and one crow who would fight to the verbal death to be right about something. Just so that he could at the end of his intolerable, insufferable chattering wink at his defeated non debating opponent. That's what always happened. Jerry would make some wild statement, some crow would stand opposed on it's improbability, there in the middle would be the shapeless empty hours spent in the furor for nothing. And then Jerry would find a spot to insert the death blow of his logic leaving those standing before him either confused or more likely tired of the fiasco a crazed crow needlessly started. Their limp stares invite his wink of judgment. She'd seen it too many times before.

"I don't know what they call themselves. I never bothered to introduce myself. I do know that the humans that have them on their farms call them 'horses'. "

Hamer interrupted. "What's a farm?"

"It's like you have here in this amusement zoo. But on a farm, the animals have to do something for or with the humans." Hamer looked at Garland who looked to Fret who looked back over to Hamer. Jerry continued, knowing he'd captured his audience. "Hey. You guys have no clue how easy you have it. These horses have to give their humans rides on their backs!"

Fret interrupted. "Who's back? The human or the horse?"

"WHAT!?"

Garland agreeable to the idea stepped into it. "Yeah, because I can't see a horse on a human back unless the horse is really small. You didn't mention how big these horses are so Fret's question is fair. Who's back?"

Hamer looked over to Peter and shrugged a convenient confusion. "It's true he didn't say how big."

Jerry had to stop the hemorrhaging idea taking over his story. "Guys, the horses are your size. The humans ride on the horse's backs. More importantly again, they have no stripes. There's cows there, too."

"What's a cow?"

"They are rather like a horse, but shorter. Stout. You could say they are stumpy horses with horns."

"Do they have stripes?"

"What? No! Only you have stripes that's my point." Jerry was feeling confident he'd gotten them in line to his logic. Which was a mistake. Paulie stopped chewing and listening, then swallowed. Paulie was Zed's second in herd. He'd learned long ago the more a creature talked, the less they knew. And this crow was talking so fast he ran into himself.

"So there's a farm where stripe less zebras called horses live with humans and stumpy horses called cows. The stripe less zebras called horses allow the humans to ride on their backs for no good reason and the stumpy horses called cows don't have stripes but have to do something with or for the human. Is that what you've just tried to say?"

Jerry paused. He wasn't sure if he liked this guy's tone at all. "Yes. Yes, you've got it. Enough, I suppose."

"I'm quite interested in cows now. Do tell. If you can make sense out of that I can accept that there are creatures called horses that give rides to humans on their backs. Do tell about the cows."

"Well fine. If you need that much information than here it is. Cows can do three things. They can make more cows. They can be eaten. And some cows let the humans take their milk by attaching them to a giant machine with hoses that suck the milk RIGHT out of them!"

"That's it! That is it! Stop talking. Do you have rabies? Did you hit your head when you landed? Is their some form of insanity in your family?" Garland again looked to Hamer to facilitate the next round of name calling.

"You're not very smart are you crow?" Hamer looked to Garland with a nod. He delivered that punch on target!

"What's smart got to do with there being three things cows can do?!" Jerry raised his voice in exasperation. How did one simple statement about having no stripes end up this awkward.

His voice grabbed his audience's attention as well as Jack's. He'd lighted on the wrong side of the commotion but was close enough to hear Jerry had chosen the wrong creatures to try to debate. He was known to do this from time to time. Jack stayed put laughing quietly. He'd like to see how Jerry came close to winning this idea of cows and horses. Jill's voice entered the fray.

"Gentlemen!" Her female voice of reason and last nerve cut through the mumbling debaters. "Does it really matter a wit about cows and horses? Garland, Hamer, Fret, Peter and Paulie are their cows or horses here?"

"No. There are not."

"Then why argue about a thing you have nothing to do with in your life?"

The zebras looked to each other for clarity to Jill's question.

"Jerry! Why do this now? We are here to find Jack and I'm not interested in listening to you stir up concerns that do not need stirring because you find it entertaining because you are actually bored with your wandering and dazed lifestyle."

Jerry looked to each of the zebras for help. They resumed foraging trying to leave the area as quickly as possible. Even a zebra can tell when a girl has had quite enough of boys. Jill stood looking Jerry's direction waiting for him to answer. As the herd walked away they walked around Jack. And there, the three stood together again after seasons apart. But Jill was too busy waiting for Jerry to explain himself. She did not notice Jack. Jerry was too busy trying to find something else to see or do, and was glad to look right into Jack's face.

"JACK! Whoa! Am I glad to see you!" He hopped and landed closer to Jack for protection. Jack laughed and shook his head.

"Yeah, you look glad to see just about anybody right now."

Jill's eyes gave away more than any words she could conjure. She flew into Jack, knocking him down with her relief and joy. She didn't realize how much she missed him until she found him. Jack hopped back up from his tackled crow position. The three stood there in the breezy sunshine of a zebra enclosure not knowing what to say. They grinned knowing good friends don't need words to say what needs saying.

"Jill I am so glad you're here! When Ardon told me he heard from Petra and Setra that you were here trying to find me, well that was great because I can't tell you how many times and places and things I've wanted to share with you. I've missed you."

"Of course you have. I missed you too. And Jerry, I somewhat missed you a little. Maybe."

Jerry wasn't fooled one bit. He knew she missed him. Maybe not the things he did, but she missed him. Jerry missed them. A slight rush of ache overwhelmed his heart just a bit. He missed Todd, too. And if he was going to admit Todd he may as well as admit the fact he missed home. And all that was in it.

"I almost missed you, too, Jill. Did you get to eat the foods over at the roller coaster yet?" He wasn't comfortable with all this emotional weight. He was hungry.

"Yes, I've been there Jerry. And I've been around meeting a few of your friends. Jack your mom misses you. The flock misses you, are you coming back or are you going to live here? Your human looks for you every day at the yellow house. You left a big hole in the world when you left."

Jack was surprised by the idea his human would miss him at all. What with the ducks and ibis and blue jays and all the parrots in the house. He was under the impression a trained human would either forget or have better things to do.

"Have you been to the tree then? Did you visit her on the back porch? Are the shells still there?"

"I've been to the tree. I met Stiltz there to start this trip to find you. I haven't visited her or the porch so I have no idea about the shells. But I've seen her come out and look right in the tree to find you. I thought she even looked at me once. Stiltz eats in the back yard with his flock, so he'd know more than me about it all."

Jack shook his head in wonder. Wow. A human missed a crow. Is that possible? It must be if Jill says she's seen it. Did his human feel the same way about him as he did about Jill all this time away? That would change everything in his mind. Would she be as happy to see him as Jill was to see him when he goes home? The thought slipped out of his mind with such ease it caught him off guard. When I go home. He'd not thought on it one way or the other, but there it was. A decision already made. But when? And why?

"Okay. Can we take this reunion business to a location with food?"

Jill laughed at Jerry. Primal urges. That's Jerry. "Let's. We're here together now. We may as well enjoy ourselves together. I'm hungry, too."

"Did you come to find me to drag me back home Jill?"

"Jack, you are your own crow. You do what you want. I just wanted to know you were safe and happy and also if you got the answers you were looking for in all this wandering. Your dad is convinced you are looking for answers. Your mom thinks you can't control wandering at all. Like a wild wind under your wings you just have to ride it out."

"Wow! What deep thoughts and ideas and words. I would almost care about all this if you two would do this deep word stuff where there is food!" Jerry's discomfort multiplied with every vulnerable thought.

They were about to take flight for the sake of one hungry crow when Zed walked around the boulder.

He shook his mane and cleared his nose from all the dust and dirt he'd inhaled grazing on grass. "Hello Jerry. Jack. I heard about your friend looking for you. I'm glad you've found each other. Now you're a murder again. Missing pieces leave spaces no one knows what to do with but walk around'."

The four discussed things Zed felt Jill needed to hear. Once a zebra believes they have a meaningful idea to share, you just have to sit down and let them finish their thoughts. Zed, being a herd leader for years, felt strongly about meaningful ideas. Jerry hopped over to the the base of the tree nearby to hunt red worms and beetles. This could take a while. Jack and Jill shared their attention and space with their good friend with a different viewpoint. The breezes picked up as the noon day turned over on itself to release it's heat into the atmosphere. Soon the clouds would find each other to form deeper clouds that would produce the perfect rain storm. As the clouds melded new clouds and weather formations, three friends formed new ideas joining different viewpoints. One outlier argued with a beetle that was not quite ready to die for another's hunger.

"GAH!" Jerry coughed, choked and spat out the beetle who closed it's wings fully now that it offloaded a dose of self defense right into the back of Jerry's throat.

"Swallow THAT crow creature!"

The stink beetle crawled into the thickest patch of long grasses disappearing from sight. His scent and taste would linger long after his exit.

"Why you continue to try to eat the beetles with stripes and long wonky antennae I will never understand." Zed spoke over the heads of Jill and Jack to Jerry. That crow would choke on a stink bug once a week. So consistent on those attempts Zed was beginning to wonder if Jerry had built a taste for their nasty flavoring.

"This is a matter of principle Zed. If I want to eat a bug, I should be able to eat that bug. That's my job. My job in this world is to eat bugs, unless there's a burrito. Then I'll eat that and save some for Terrance. How would you feel if the grass bit you back and said, no, you can't eat me. You'd be insulted Zed. You would be personally insulted and you know it."

"Jerry I think you choke on stink bugs for the opportunity to complain about stink bugs."

*****

The crows found themselves on the edge of a sidewalk, standing in the trimmed grass looking up. The human count was low. The rains coming off the gulf were keeping them away it seemed. Those that did walk by carried no food, just umbrellas and the occasional drink of differing flavors. None of which would satisfy a hungry crow named Jerry. Jerry was looking for the food the children would eat. They ate the best flavors. And they shared without hesitation. Unlike their accompanying adult humans who did not notice a starving crow any more than their own untied shoe. Clueless, like the farmer who got him in all that trouble with the squirrel. Jerry flexed the feathers on his neck thinking on that squirrel. And that farmer and that whole fiasco. "This isn't working. Let's go over to the other side of the place where the kids pet goats."

Jill sighed. Goats? Kids petting goats. Did she dare ask any questions at all. Jack didn't while he took flight to head in the direction of the goats. There were chickens there, but Jack assumed Jerry had a plan to counter all that negativity. Jerry followed Jack's tac while Jill paused long enough to take note of a dove on the roof of a small building on the other side of the sidewalk. Doves always looked so relaxed. She bolted into the air to follow her two friends looking forward to their first adventure as three friends. It had been a long time since they had just been three friends.

Jill caught up with the boys and slipped between them to shout a question to Jerry. "What's a goat?"

"It's like a horse with horns! But smaller."

"Wouldn't it be easier to say they are like a cow, but smaller?"

"If you had met a cow you'd know that can't be true."

Jack turned slightly in the winds to catch a draft down toward the roof of a large red building. Below and surrounding that building were dozens of children. Jerry cut right underneath Jill and fell in behind Jack, while Jill dipped to take the third spot. They landed on the roof without a sound. Jerry and Jack hopped to the edge of the roof to look over and down on the scene.

Jill hopped to another roof edge to look over. She smelled grasses and earth and something new. Goat. Not that far off from the smell of a dog park filled with panting drooling dogs. She saw what had to be goats wondering in directions that led to children with hands filled with food offerings.

"Jerry, I think goats are like dogs."

"Goats don't chase balls, Jill."

She hopped to the boys side of the roof to look over. She heard the voices before she could focus on the creatures. They were girls and they were busy disagreeing on everything. Quickly. What she saw didn't match what she heard. Birds, birds walking, scratching and walking more. They endlessly paced and searched the ground with their large scratching claws. When they walked their heads led the way at each step and pulled back to again move forward pointing their beak in the direction of their feet. The chatter carried to the roof and lost itself in the winds.

"There's no point in trying to explain her. She's her own chicken."

"I'm not trying to explain her. I'm trying to explain her sister."

"Really! Same difference."

"No, no it's not. Have you met her sister?"

They rooted and scratched and chattered in small circles. When a child entered their area, they scattered like frogs in a bog. But not so far away as to miss the foods the child would throw toward them. Once the child stopped throwing food they would eat the offerings and continue defending their poultry positions.

"I didn't know she had a sister."

"Of course! He mother hatched four eggs that summer."

"If they are from the same nest I can't see how any difference could result."

"You think too much Ann."

"I do not!"

"Yes, you do. Have you ever thought about not thinking so much?"

"That is a trick question I am not falling for today Marie."

"Lynn! Lynn, tell her. Tell Ann your sister is just like you. There's no difference."

Lynn stuck her head out of the chicken coop to look at the crowds and her friends. Ann and Marie would take hours to disagree only to forget what they didn't agree on in the first place. The crowds were smaller today. Which worked for Lynn. Staying safe from scurrying child feet was more work than it was worth in scratch feed. Better to wait for less of them, then eat. "My sister is not just like me. She's just like my other sisters. I am not like any of them. I told you both this long ago. I hatched from the winter nest, they hatched from the spring nest. I barely know them!"

"Ha!" Ann threw her head back and let out one good chicken 'bokka bok'. She looked at Marie. Marie yanked her head back and forth and went back to scratching the ground while pecking for tossed foods.

"That doesn't mean a thing to my point. I'm done with this conversation. You are both beyond stubborn. You're practically roosters!"

She walked up the wooden ramp to go back into the chicken coop. It was quiet in there. Lynn's sisters were sitting and she'd clear up this point with them. She didn't need Ann or Lynn to know for a fact that a chicken can only be like their mother. It's the way of things. Roosters are like their fathers. That's the way of things. Why these two disagreed on the bare facts of life was beyond her. Marie took her position in her own nest box third level up, above Garnet and to the right of Cindy.

"Ladies! Are you, or are you not, just like your sister Lynn?"

The sitting hens looked at each other and then over and up to Marie. Garnet stood to look at her brood of eggs beneath her. She rolled each egg half way over, and turned herself half way round to face the wall, and sat carefully back onto her clutch. "You've far too much time on your hands, Marie. Why don't you just go lay an egg."

Jerry flew off the roof without a word to land on the fencing surrounding the goats. Listening to chickens was not something he enjoyed for any length of time. Jack and Jill flew in and landed not far away on the same fence. The goats were milling about the enclosure. There were fainting goats, Nubian goats and three regular goats. The three never fainted. Nor did they jump like the Nubian goats. They wondered the hay covered floor quietly with purpose. Jerry had never learned what their purpose was, but they looked purposeful doing it.

The goat area was set up for access through the fencing itself. The openings of wire were big enough for the smaller children to reach through with fistfuls of goat chow. The fence was low enough so that taller children or their parents could reach over and down to the waiting goats with open hands filled with goat chow.

There were water bottles hanging from walls for the goats. Some were lower to the ground for the miniature goats and baby goats of the regular goats, and higher up for the fainting goats and regular goats. The flooring was covered in hay, the hay was intermittently matted with goat waste. In the open air the smell was barny, farmy and earthy. Jill's opinion of wet dog smells weren't too far off from wrong. If the dog were a goat.

A fainting goat ran over to stand under Jerry and look up. He was so very excited to see his friend. "Jerry!" and he fainted.

Jill looked at Jerry in surprise. "Well aren't you going to help your friend?"

"Wait on it."

Jack's concern lay in the fact that the other goats had run over to greet Jerry but they too seemed overwhelmed. Now there was a pile of unconscious goats, legs sticking in all directions. "Jerry! Do something. They're your friends for crow's sake!"

"Wait on it, Jack. They're fine."

The remaining goats stepped around and sometimes over their stiff laid out goat mates. They were as unimpressed as Jerry over the scene. Jill looked to Jack for some sort of interpretation. Jack shrugged. Per usual with Jerry some things have no reason.

The first goat down was the first to come back to life. Sadly, he was on the bottom of the stiffened pile of goats that fell after him. He kicked and pushed and head butted his way to the top. With each effort he roused his inert friends. A cascade of waking goats struggled against each other to find their feet and bearings.

Some fainted a second time inside the struggling mass of goat. Others called out sheepishly. Awkward at best, but obviously embarrassed on the whole.

As the last fainted goat came back from the stupefied and one last goat stood swooning it seemed the event was over.

"Jerry! It's so good to see you again! You brought friends, too. This is amazing!"

"Whoa, slow down Rutt, I'd hate to see you fall into another coma. It's really good to see you, too. This is Jack and Jill."

"Hello Jack and Jill welcome to the goat barn! Rutt stood tall and stiffen. He just couldn't help himself, or his blood pressure." Rutt fell to the left, out cold.

The other goats walked around him and to the fence line to be caressed and fed. One little goat passed out on the way to a smallish child with a fistful of chow. He'd stepped on a mouse. It was too much.

"This is all just sad. Really. Is this their plight? Is this why they exist to randomly fall over in a daze?"

Jerry smiled without looking at her. Whys. She was more obsessed with them than Jack ever was. And she didn't even realize it. "Wait on it. Goats are the best for bringing in the kids with food."

"I'm not eating goat food, Jerry. Look what it does to them!"

"No, they bring their own food in here with them. Just wait on it." Jerry turned around on the fence top to look at benches lined up across the sidewalk. The benches faced the goat enclosure. At the end of each bench was a goat chow dispenser. A child would insert a coin, turn a knob and hold their hands under an opening so the chow fell into their hands. They didn't catch all the chow all the time. This left remnants for wondering ducks, chickens and local blue jays to snatch up.

The wondering ducks and chickens wanted nothing to do with the humans. They infiltrated and snatched from behind the benches to retreat under fencing surrounding trees and flowering bushes. Jack looked up and realized there was a roof that ran the length of the sidewalk. There, doves, robins, and starlings perched on the rafters. They too were on the hunt for leftovers and tasty bits of morsels humans were known to reject or carelessly drop.

Jack noticed just how careless humans were about food after he'd come to this place. They dropped it. Threw it down. Threw it in cans. Held it until they forgot they were trying to hold it. And sometimes they passed their food to another human who tasted it and passed it to yet another. But sooner or later one of them would throw it down. Throw it in a can or just drop it. As if there was some endless supply of things. Humans didn't seem as concerned with finding more of it. Humans didn't seem concerned with anything except, more. They wondered quickly, always pointing to where they hadn't yet arrived.

They were always missing everything because they were always looking for something that wasn't there yet. Not crow at all. A crow was careful and aware. A good crow shared when he had more than he needed. A good crow left some behind for another who may show up later. A crow took the time to notice everything. Mostly because if you were there, you may as well act like it.

Jill flew up into the rafters to chat with a dove. They were a peaceful group, there had to be a reason why.

"We choose not to pay attention to things that make no sense." Darla nestled deeper into her sitting position on the rafter. Her eyes softened into a smile for Jill. Poor dear. Crows tended to mind all the business all the time. They just lied to themselves about doing it. Her question was honest enough. Why do doves always look so relaxed? It's a good question if you aren't a dove.

Jill took a deep breath and looked out from her position on the rafter to take in all the commotion created by so many different beings sharing one small space. Her mind posited; How do you know when something isn't making sense? Just because it doesn't make sense to a crow doesn't mean it doesn't make sense to, say, a human. She was being a bit silly here. Humans rarely make sense. More rarely than making sense, they were notable in never making a point.

"Has choosing what doesn't make sense ever gone wrong on you? For example, what you thought didn't make sense actually does. You chose to ignore it and then relaxed only to have that come back and be a problem?" Jill looked to Darla, waiting. She felt she had constructed the question clearly enough for a good answer.

"You miss the point Jill. If I choose to believe it does not make sense, then it does not. And I move on to the better things." Jill felt a rush of realization scamper down her spine into her tail feathers. She stood up in her perched position. She turned her head to gaze on a sincerely tranquil dove named Darla.

"And if a fellow dove does not agree with you?"

Darla grinned inside her composed place answering in a quiet voice. "A fellow dove would never think to say such a thing out loud. You can't move onto your better things if you are busy considering others choices."

They shared their rafter in silence. Darla content in her decisions. Jill on fire reveling in these new ideas which all made complete sense. Darla felt Jill's relaxed company. She opened one eye to take a look at a crow not concerned with all the business. "You know Jill, you ought to ask the hens about that other matter you're thinking on lately."

"The other matter? How do you know I have another matter? I mean, I do. But I didn't say anything about it!"

"Every one has another matter, dear. You should go ask the hens. They are quite helpful really."

"They seem a bit disagreeable though."

"You can disagree without being disagreeable, Jill. Go on then, go get that last matter settled. Don't worry about your friends. I'll keep an eye on them. They're busy down there with those two boys and the hotdogs they hold. That will take a bit of time to finish."

Jill looked down and saw the boys negotiating with two human boys. Darla smiled through her sleepy eyes. "Go, dear. Hotdogs and boys have never solved a matter yet."

All the hens were out of the chicken coop scratching and pecking at the ground. The gate was closed leaving all the humans on the other side allowing a few hours to themselves. They clucked, bokked and scratched through passing thoughts and shared ideas spoken through beaks filled with grains.

"I wouldn't eat a live bug. I might eat a deceased bug. But only if he just died. Not one that had laid out in the sun for days drying up."

Ann's truth burst into the quiet scratches of a group of hens. No one had brought up bugs as a suggestion. No one had pointed out a freshly dead bug or one drying up in the sun. Ann offered up this truth because she felt others would benefit from hearing it. All the hens stopped stepping and scratching. They paused on Ann's thought and looked to the sky, or rather the roof blocking the sky and considered her truth.

"Well I doubt a child would offer a fistful of bugs, dead or alive, for us anyway. I doubt their parents would allow them to hold a bug, dead or alive. I wouldn't worry about that idea." Marie was the best at breaking down ideas into their most pliable and applicable points.

"If I was a rooster I wouldn't be so rude as to wake everybody at the crack of dawn." Lynn paused her scratch waiting for the girls to respond. Her truth was obvious.

"If you were a rooster you couldn't help yourself. You'd have to be a hen pretending to be a rooster to help yourself." Kimmy didn't bother pausing her scratching. Genius stood out no matter what was going on around it.

'What are you saying to me? That I can't control myself?"

"No Lynn. I'm saying if you were a rooster you wouldn't be yourself. You would be a rooster. And none of them can control themselves."

Lynn and Kimmy looked to each other and waited for the other to disagree. No disagreements were forthcoming.

They resumed scratching in a concerted effort.

The hens again scratched in random circles. Jill landed to the left of one circle consisting of Lynn, Marie, and Kimmy. No hen reacted to her arrival. Jill waited to be noticed. She wasn't. The hens continued their circling foraging by enlarging the circle around and past Jill. She was forced to follow them to the other side of the area they called home. "Excuse me ladies."

Marie looked up in shock. She waited for Garnet to do something. When it came to visitors Garnet knew what to do. Garnet stopped scratching and scampered over to Jill. "And you are?"

"I am Jill Crow. Darla sent me."

Garnet looked over her shoulder to Marie. Another one. They were going to have to talk to Darla again about sending visitors. As if they had time for all this talking about things not chicken. Garnet took a breath and smiled resolutely at their visitor. "What questions have you asked Darla can't answer?"

"I didn't. I mean, she answered my questions just fine. We weren't talking about any particular thing when she suggested I should see you hens. She seems to think you might help me about a matter I haven't thought about." Jill felt awkward about all this now.

Here she was standing in the middle of a chicken place with hens busy with their own business and she had no clear reason to be there at all. Apologizing and leaving felt appropriate. But then that would be rude now that's she's interrupted their day.

How does one extract themselves from a conversation that hadn't started, but hadn't yet ended? She waited. Maybe the hens knew.

Lynn signaled the other girls to join Garnet with the visiting crow. The sooner they attend to things, the sooner they could get back to doing what they set out to do. Jill watched as the others approached and stepped back to give room, for escape. These ladies seemed safe enough, but their numbers were growing. Garnet waited for her flock to settle in and scratch and listen. Chickens can not stand still. It's not in their make up. Scratching claws tend to fuel the brain of chickens. The more scratching going on, the more thinking. So the saying goes.

"Darla is too kind. We're just a group of girls getting by in life. Aren't all girls?" Garnet seemed to be asking her friends this question rather than Jill. Again, Jill felt that awkward outlier feeling.

"I'm not sure. I only know crow girls myself. I've not met too many other types of girls to know. I suppose we are all just trying to get by in life. It doesn't matter if you are a boy or a girl."

This set the hens off laughing. Garnet knew what Darla wanted this crow to know.

"Of course it matters if you are a boy or a girl! Boys just do things without caring about much other than what they can see in front of their nose. Girls have to think about everything else before they can think about caring about what they see in front of their nose. And by the time they get done with everything else, they don't care. They are just tired!"

Jill looked down at her feet. She looked up to Garnet's waiting gaze. She didn't have a response. But she did have an emotion. She felt like shouting YES! She hadn't quite decided why. Her whole self wanted to point right at Garnet, jump up and down in place while shouting YES YES YES! She held herself quiet for the moment. The other hens leaned into the circle, eyes wide. They all wondered the same thing. Does this crow understand?

"Are you saying this is the matter I hadn't thought about yet?"

Garnet sighed. Why do they all work so hard at not accepting the fact that boys and girls are different, that boys don't care until they meet the right girl. And when the boy meets the right girl, the girl is still left handling everything else until they are exhausted? What is so not clear about this clarity? Why did Darla send this women to her so clueless. She could at least throw out a few statistics to support the truth she and her hen friends were expected to reveal.

"Jill I'm saying your matter is boy and girl expectations. Your matter is how you react to it. Truth is you don't have to accept it. You don't have to be anything other than you. Now that you stand here with us I can see where you are stuck."

"I'm stuck?"

"You're stuck girl."

"Here?"

"In the ethereal sense, yes."

Jill looked into the expectant eyes of chickens who knew, waiting on her to know. Chickens twitch, a lot. They stood twitching heads and scratching feet. Their quiet clucking felt, comforting. In a foreigner in a strange land way.

"What if I didn't know I was stuck until now and now that I know I'm stuck, I'm still not sure that's the matter?"

The hens twitched while looking at each other. They weren't going to say one word to that, not one. Best to leave it to Garnet to sort out. Whatever that crow just said made their collective brain hurt.

"Well then, we've just wasted quite a bit of foraging time then, haven't we?"

With that the hens disbanded their attention and locations moving off into their quiet cycling of foraging. They were done offering what they had to give. It was up to their visitor to accept the gift or leave it behind. It was not their responsibility to feed her by mouth.

Jill felt the loss of company before they began circling away. She flew to a rafter further down the roof to mull all this out. While watching the boys visiting goats. Why was she even watching boys with goats? Why was she on the other side of her world anyway? Why had she felt so driven to know what Jack was doing and how he was doing while doing it? The questions cascaded down her brain like rain. They left a puddle of an answer, a totality of the truth. Jill Crow was avoiding her own life. She was as the chickens surmised, worrying about everything else first, leaving her exhausted for her own. She moved her gaze away from the boys and their goats. She rested her mind on the horizon just exposed below the rim of the porch roof itself. So much horizon.

*****

Rutt and Tuke stood shoulder to shoulder as they do most days. Jerry stood ground in front of them. The three laughed with the ease that old friends share. "And then I left it on the front porch right where they'd never expect!"

The goats roared with laughter at that idea. As much as goats can roar. They were more baying a goaty gurgle enjoying the punchline of a very good joke. Jerry told good jokes. They were good because they were real stories. That's the important part of a good joke, it should be about a real place and time. And it should end where no one listening would ever go.

"So, how's things on the farm then?"

"We don't spend too much time out there anymore. We live here mostly. But farmer comes by quite a bit to check up on us. He brings that hay we like from the field behind the barn."

Tuke chimed in, "I love that hay."

"You like it here. Being petted and fed by little humans?"

"All in all being fed by little humans isn't bad."

Tuke chimed in, "They smell funny though."

"Yes. Little humans smell. They can't help it. They're so low to the ground they pick up everything stinky."

Tuke chimed in again, "On purpose."

"Yes, they do pick up stinky things on purpose."

Jerry laughed with his friends. He missed these goats. It had been far too long and quite a nice surprise to find them here at all. He'd met them when they were younger at the farm with the squirrel that ended up hating him, and the farmer that couldn't remember a simple order for dinner. Thinking on the good things of the farm helped him forget about the prickly bad things.

"I have a theory about the little humans."

Rutt looked at Tuke and then to Jerry. He was genuinely shocked any creature would take the time to consider anything about humans. They weren't very smart, so that explained quite a lot right there.

"Do tell your theory!"

Jerry looked over his shoulder and around the place as if he were about to reveal a magnificent secret. The fainting goats were laying down now, all in a corner asleep. The miniature goats were in the goat barn hiding from the small humans. When you were a miniature goat small anything felt too big. The children lined up at the goat fence were busy eating their own food at the benches across the way. He could reveal his secret.

Jack perched above him on the fencing. Listening. "Yeah, Jerry. What's your theory? I know they are great for begging lunch from, but is there more?"

"Thank you for asking Jack! I was told this story by a great beast I met when I first visited here. An Orangutan by the name of Tanner. He had quite a few ideas about humans, small and large. He gave all this quite a bit of thought."

The day Jerry learned the ideas of an orangutan named Tanner, Tanner had just arrived after a long flight on a plane with three humans attending him. To say Tanner was not in the best frame of mind would be to say your luggage waiting for you at the carousel would enjoy another flight, just for fun. Tanner sat at the top of a tree house built by not orangutans. It wasn't tall enough. And it was flat in more places than not. Specifically it was not a 40 foot tree Tanner preferred. It was a 10 foot platform made from a 40 foot tree. It was all obscene. They had left a pile of fruit and vegetables for him to eat on the platform. This would be the positive reinforcement referred to so often back at the other place with the 12 foot platform made from a 30 foot tree. It was all obscene there as well.

Tanner sat staring at the food he didn't have to find, sitting on the platform he didn't have to climb looking out into the faces of the species that felt it important to attempt this idea of whatever this idea was in their head. He didn't feel threatened. He also didn't feel comfortable with all the assumptions built to create a human's idea of what an orangutan's life added up to be. His boredom and disdain percolated. It was precisely that boredom and slight disdain that allowed one black crow to get his attention. He would never have paid any mind to a bird back in the forest. And they would not have chosen his company either. There's no reason for either of them to discuss anything. And yet today, sitting 10 foot above the ground this particular crow landed on one of the stumps of the 40 foot tree cut to size. And he seemed quite pleased with himself by doing it.

"Hello orange ape! I am Jerry. I'm new around here. I just flew in."

Tanner looked at the crow, and reached out to grab a durian fruit. Ripe and smelly as only a durian fruit could be.

"Whoa! Are you going to eat that on purpose? That smells like dead turtle eggs left in the sun, next to a bog filled with dead turtles."

Tanner bit off a section of skin, to insert his leathery fingers into the fruit opening the durian into two halves. He deftly pulled a section of fruity meat from one half and slipped it between his teeth. He chewed slowly sitting back on his platform to take in a crow with no manners whatsoever.

"You seem to be enjoying that stink fruit quite a bit. I take it your nose is broken?"

"My nose is not broken bird, but neither are my ears. An unfortunate place to be at this moment."

Jerry was determined to ignore words he didn't enjoy. He would let them roll right through his left ear and out the right. No point in letting words get in the way of understanding. "You just arrived then? Me, too! I have a flock on the other side of the bay. They don't get out much. I take it upon myself to experience life, go back home and share my experiences and then go back out again to get more."

Tanner didn't reply, he chewed his durian slowly. Letting the sweetness slide over his taste buds. Durian fruit was a fist fight for your face. Your nose believed one thing, and your taste buds believed another about it. Eating durian fruit relied on the eater choosing sides and sticking with that decision. Tanner licked his fingers after dropping the other half of the large piece into his mouth. He exhaled through his mouth so as not to smell the fruit in reverse. That too, was an integral component to successfully enjoying durian fruit. "Bird. I find you less annoying than the humans on the other side of that fence. You don't need to take that as a compliment."

Jerry jumped off the section of platform to land on a stump closer to the great ape. He could smell the durian less, up wind. "They aren't that bad. The little ones are less bad than the big ones. I'll say that."

Tanner broke another durian section away from it's pod. "The little ones become the big ones eventually. I prefer to dislike them evenly, since they all treat me as some object. They aren't that smart. At all." The ape chewed thoughtfully on the section careful to breath through his mouth. Discussing humans was already a distasteful exercise.

"How long have you been dealing with humans? I don't have to deal, I just fly away if they seem too interested in what I'm doing. Which is not me bragging. I consider being a flighted creature a luck of the draw."

Tanner swallowed with an exhale careful to keep his nose out of it. "I've been among them for many seasons now. I was snatched from the last tree in my forest home. One tree left, me at the top of it watching monsters and machines destroying everything I knew. A very bad day. Worst of my life. Now. I'm bored. I'm bored and I don't feel quite well. I don't do much, as there's nothing to do. What am I supposed to do with this broken tree turned into some human thing? It was like this at the last place with the last broken tree turned into something I sat on. Nothing to do but ignore the hordes of humans wondering back and forth, listening to shouts of humans telling me to turn around so they could see my face. Why they wanted to see my face just plain irritates me. I don't want to see theirs. Now I'm here, and it's not much different than there, and I can't remember home very well anymore. It's all quite debilitating. And there they all are, behind you staring at me. As if I'm the one that's odd. I can't bare to look at them anymore. Do you know their problem? They have a big problem that they can't seem to accept."

Jerry thought a minute on the question. He felt confident with his answer. "They aren't that smart!"

"No. No that's part of the problem. They are that smart. Which makes all of this you and I sit inside of pathetic and wrong and unjust. They are that smart, they choose not to be. On purpose. As an excuse to do the things they want rather than doing the things that should be done. The young ones aren't that smart. But they become that smart and then they too choose not to be, to be able to make the choices that are wrong. I have never in all my jungle days met a creature that willfully lies to itself every single day.

And to train their young, they teach them to believe their own lies and then send them out to create their own personal lies. You can't do much with a creature that believes it's own lies. You have to wait for them to destroy themselves. It'll take awhile I'm afraid."

Jerry felt helplessness wash over his thoughts. He couldn't think of another creature motived to lie to itself. It made no sense to do it. It was just plain stupid. Which long way round proved they aren't that smart! But just saying they aren't that smart didn't cover the depth of their own delirium. "Are you saying they will die lying to themselves? Is that what you are saying? They will tell themselves and each other lies to get what they want when what they want will wipe them out?"

"Yes. And they'll take us with them, too."

"Well, I don't want to go."

"Bird you don't have a choice. We'll die first anyway. I've already lost my home and family. Now I'm in this place waiting to die."

"Ape! You're a little depressing. I mean, you've got the food you like, plenty of time to think, freedom to …walk around and ape a little. No one will cut anything down around you now. You get a lot of freedoms without worrying about things trying to eat you in the wild. At least you know what will happen tomorrow."

"At least is a horrible place to live. Tomorrow doesn't matter when at least is all you have."

"Okay, well, what of the little humans, isn't there some hope in them? You said they don't lie to themselves. Maybe they might stop the bigger ones."

"They have no influence. I have observed on many occasions the larger humans literally ignoring their young. They poke at something in their hand and keep their eyes on this thing. They barely talk or teach their young. Sometimes they hold that thing in their hand up and look at it rather than me. Then they poke it. Then they show each other their thing and laugh. In fact, none of them look directly at me much. They look at that thing in their hand, and then show it to each other. They are so, odd.

But the little ones don't do this, they look directly at me. I can look into their eyes and know they see me. But the older ones, the bigger ones, do not instruct their young. The small ones only know what they see. If I chose to speak their language I would tell the young to run. Nothing good will come of listening to the larger ones. Just, run."

Tanner looked down at the durian in his hand and tossed it away. He'd lost his appetite again. That was happening more often than not lately.

Jerry looked over his shoulder at the humans of all sizes walking past Tanner's space. Some paused to hold up the thing in their hands. Some looked away to other spaces while their young stood on their toes to look over the railing at Tanner. The railing was a lie. It did not keep Tanner inside. It kept the humans out. Jerry started on this thought. Who was behind a fence and who was in front? Tanner sensed the crow's change of thoughts.

"They look like the ones controlled by bars and fences, don't they? And they don't realize it at all. They herd closer and tighter than any animal I have seen. These humans prefer being told where to go and when. And I believe if you are one of the unlucky creatures trapped in one of these places, they believe creatures prefer being told where to go and when. Because they do not know what freedom is, bird. They do not know they are walking between fences keeping them out. They herd mindlessly carrying a mindless thing with them. It seems to sedate them."

Jerry watched them walk by and saw the mindlessness clearly now that Tanner mentioned it. He saw the young learn the mindlessness. He saw one older human hand their thing to a smaller human. The moment the child held it, he turned away from Tanner. As if while holding this thing, nothing else mattered. The adults were teaching the young not to notice anything. Jerry turned to Tanner shocked at the truth.

"They aren't that smart because they chose not to be. But worse, they choose not to help their young!"

Rutt and Tuke gasped in their own experience of this truth. They looked at Jerry, and then to each other.

Jack didn't wait to argue a point. "I know a human that chooses to know the truth of it. She's not like any of that you are talking about!"

Jerry turned toward Jack in slight disappointment. He'd worked hard to tell this story to end at that last line at just the right pace for affect and shock. Tanner is a great story, and a better ending and Jack had ruined it completely with his human bragging. Now his story was lost to Jack's human idea.

Rutt looked to Jack wanting to hear more about this human of his, certainly there had to be one or seven of them that weren't completely lost. Rutt and Tuke knew 3 personally. They came to visit every Sunday and brought strawberries, just for them! Rutt and Tuke didn't even ask! They just did it with kindness and understanding. And the best head scratches! So that was four humans. There had to be more of them out there. "Who's this human of yours Jack?"

"She's my father's first, and then I claimed the house and tree and her for my own family. When and if I have a family. She's quite kind. And aware of her own less than creature status. She feeds every creature that shows up to visit her. She's thoughtful. She's humble."

Rutt and Tuke looked at each other and back at Jack. "We have three like that here. They give me hope that they all aren't so lost."

Jerry stood frustrated as to how his dramatic storytelling had been sucked dry by all this happy blappy business. He could bring up a squirrel and a farmer and fix their attitudes. But then Rutt and Tuke would remind him it's their farmer he was slandering. It just didn't pay to deliver good drama.

"Okay. I'm bored. Let's go find a snack over at the bench where the little ones are dropping food."

"You go ahead Jerry. I need to talk to Jill. I see her up in the rafters."

"Okay, Jack. But that kid over their has bologna. It looks slathered with mustard, too."

"It's all yours Jerry. We'll catch up."

Jerry flew up into the air to land at the feet of the bologna sandwich eating child. The boy ripped off a chunk of crust and threw it barely missing Jerry's head. There was no bologna with it. He looked at the human and at the mustard covered crust. It would be one of those days.

*****

Jack bid farewell to Rutt and Tuke. He wasn't sure if they noticed his departure as they became quite busy head butting each other. He flew up and over to Jill's roost spot in the rafters. Looking out it seemed people went on forever. "Hi."

"Hi. Did I wake you?"

"No, I'm just napping really. Thinking on things a chicken said."

"Did the chicken make sense?"

"Yes. Yes she did. How did your conversation with the goats go?"

"The goats made sense, Jerry didn't."

"No matter where you go, there you are, poor Jerry. He hasn't a clue about himself."

"I think he does, which is more frightening."

Jill laughed at the truth of it all. Truth being personal. The hens weren't far off on this idea in their own right. To be that aware makes life simple. If you aren't busy lying to yourself you don't have to worry about remembering what you thought you told yourself you believed. "I think I'm going to go home, Jack. I'm tired of all this running around. I'm glad you're happy and safe. I'll tell your mom first thing."

"You always knew exactly what you were supposed to do. Even now, you are certain it's time to go home."

"Oh Jack, I don't think I know much of anything really. I don't think I've ever known. I just do the best I can when it comes time to decide. I commit. Honestly I think every one is pretending they know, when no one really knows a thing. We are so busy trying to convince each other, and ourselves, of what we think is the right answer and why we chose it in the first place. I just know I'm a bit tired of not being home. That's enough why to decide."

They watched the humans pass under them in both directions. So many of them. So many different ones. When you took the time to really look at them, you saw that no two were alike. Jack marveled at the complexity of them. "I used to have a hard time believing any bird could be so certain about anything. The Code is so specific and we're all so not the same, like them. How could one way of doing things fit us all?"

"You have a lot of your dad in you."

He smiled thinking on his father. He missed him at this very moment. "Yeah, I do. You know what I've learned with all this traveling and meeting new creatures, Jill?"

"What?"

"Nothing new.

Jill looked at Jack in shock. How could a crow go so far, see so much, meet so many and learn nothing at all? That was why he left in the first place. To find out things, if he couldn't find anything out here then no one could. Jerry was another story. If he didn't find things where he was he'd go somewhere else, and make things up to satisfy himself. If ever there was a crow that could be a human it was Jerry. But Jack, Jack was entirely too crow to be that not crow. "Nothing at all? Not one thing at all with all your adventure behind you?"

"No. I found more of the same in every creature. I found more of the same inside places that were meant to be different. I found that no matter how far you go to find something new, there you are in your own head. This has been a great adventure. I have met creatures smarter than me, and not so smart at all. I've eaten things I didn't know existed. I heard languages I didn't understand spoken by creatures that wanted the same thing as me. I went to roost tired, woke up hungry and spent the day doing what I would have done at home. It's just a bit more surprising out here, that's all.
And you know Jill, I don't think there's a why at all. There can't be one of them. There has to be many of them and they'll be different than the day before. No matter where you wake up. The trick seems to be waking up near familiar faces and places, that makes it easier. You don't go to roost so tired if you have friends nearby. You wake up better when you know you have your family waiting. I did learn that. I don't think that's new, so much as clearer."

Jill exhaled a breath of relief. She'd felt all of that her whole life, but never took the time to think it through in words. Knowing something isn't the same as identifying it. She let the words Jack spoke bob and float in her mind. Somehow she felt better for hearing them. More importantly she knew they were good honest words spoken by a friend. Jack was a very good crow. She was grateful to have him as a friend. They perched together in the same cloud of thoughts, while the hum of humans passed below like a bubbling river.

Jack felt ready to go home. Jack felt ready to be the best crow he knew, at home.

"OH MY CROW Did you see that!?!?" Jerry in his impeccable Jerry timing landed with scratching claws and beating wings on the rafter in front of Jack and Jill. He was full on Jerry.

"DID YOU SEE IT?" He was breathing fast and hard. Looking to Jill then Jack for confirmation on their participation in his current moment of chaos.

Jack looked to Jill. She to him. "No Jerry, we missed it."

"WHAT!?! How could you miss fainting goats passing out on top of a little human? It happened right down there! You couldn't even see the little human except for his hand sticking out from under all the goats that fell on him! And let me tell you once a goat faints, you might be there a while. The little human crawled under the fence to hug a goat and the next thing I see is the fainting goats just freezing up and tipping over one by one, piling up! All that's left is a little human hand sticking up in the air with a popsicle in it! There was still sticky ice on the stick, too!"

"You mean like the one in your claw right now?" Jill was embarrassed.

"Are you kidding me? I hate good tastes going to waste you know this Jill. Do not look that surprised. The little human's over there with his mom."

"Yes, he's crying because you stole his food, Jerry."

"NO Jill. He's crying because she's spitting on a thing and wiping his face with it. Good NIGHT that has to be some kind of awful thing right there. I'd rather be buried in stupefied goats than have that done to me."

The three crowed with laughter at the scene below. The goats were aware again, and at the farthest end of the pen. Gathered in horror at the sight of the human mother cleaning it's young. Who does such a thing?

"Jerry we're going to fly home today." Jack spoke after the last of the laughter faded.

"I'm going to stay behind for a while guys. These goats are hilarious. There's everything I need under this roof."

Jill smiled to herself. All was right in the world at that very moment. Crows don't take too much time on the emotional side of things. They clearly acknowledge emotions, but they don't repeat themselves, nor do they linger trying to make a bigger impression than the words create. The other crow either agrees, disagrees or has other plans. Accepting the others viewpoint without judgement makes life spin along smoothly. Crows are emotionally efficient.

Jerry flew down to the sidewalk landing in front of another child with a popsicle in hand. He'd dropped the harvested popsicle on his way down. Fresh was always better.

Jack and Jill let go of their rafter to swoop down and up again heading to the sky in search of the tail winds taking them back home. The winds were in their favor. Fall brought cooler air feeding the streams heading out toward their destination. Jack thought on the idea of the water waiting discovery further out, past home. The idea brought comfort rather than an urge. There was a certain amount of relief knowing there was more to what existed nearby. He held a new confidence in that idea. Somehow this adventure was enough to convince him that any new adventure would bring new experiences, but not necessarily new truths. His truths were true no matter where he took himself. His truths came from him. What a relief. Controlling all that chaos as a means to an end was just too much to ask of any crow.

His thoughts wandered to what he left behind. His tree, his family, the lady in the yellow house. Todd. There was an under appreciated crow. He and Jill dove under a flock of ducks meandering in the winds. Too slow, not quite certain as to what lake to drop into, they meandered quacking and calling uncertain considerations for each lake that passed underneath. Jack remembered what that felt like.

He needed to thank Todd for being a patient example of a good crow. Some crow just seemed to know enough to be satisfied with it all. Although Jill's uncertain considerations were a revelation. A crow could be quietly insecure hiding behind certainty.

He thought on that while heading back up into the cooler tail winds after he and Jill passed the ducks. It would have been helpful to know she had been so uncertain. Now that he thought on the entire flock and family, it would be better if every crow honestly stated their status.

If he'd known Jill had been that unsettled, they could have shared his wavering and her vacillating and come to a truth that took him hundreds of miles and multiple seasons to find. No one really knows. Every one doubts themselves. Except Gregory. Jack was certain that a rigorous rhino stayed honest with themselves and others. If only to save a few minutes time.

Their flight was calm and cool. The horizon from their cruising altitude lay out as wide as his sight could take in. There was a slight curve to it as every wing flap moved them forward. The horizon line changed from trees to houses, to trees to large lakes with trees and more houses. The curved horizon line never got closer, it stayed put revealing new outlines and hints of somewhere else. They flew on quietly entertaining their own thoughts while the earth rotated toward them. The atmosphere supporting their efforts of flight.

Familiarity revealed itself. Trees and houses and streets and smaller lakes were exposed with every mile flown. Home was so very close. They flew over canals wide and deep. They flew over a busy boulevard and arrived in their own airspace with little fanfare but carrying their own joy. Tinney Creek ran straight and true directly under him. Jack looked to Jill with a smile. She laughed herself a quick nose dive to get closer. Jack followed. "She's at the end of the Creek. Are we stopping?" They flew parallel over the water, the yellow house and pine tree fast approaching. Jack was surprised at his heart racing so. He felt delighted to be home. He felt relieved. The pine tree was coming up fast and Jack lifted himself to meet the tree's height. He landed on the second branch from the very top with Jill coming in onto the third. They caught their breath.

"I'm back! It feels like I've been gone forever. It doesn't even feel like all that adventure was real now."

"She's been looking for you the entire time, Jack."

"What is going on in her backyard? There's a dozen ducks, ibis, blue jay, doves …an egret!"

The gull called from above complaining over Jack's voice. Gull are whiney. They complain about everything. They complain when they're eating, not eating, sleeping, not sleeping, flying or not flying. Their own kind find themselves annoying. Gull will use human parking lots the same way they use any stretch of beach.

Word made it to the shopping are across the boulevard that a woman came outside twice a day and fed every living creature. The story started one afternoon when a black skimmer showed up in the parking lot and landed near a flock of laughing gull. It's said he was confused by the black heads from afar. Made a few presumptuous assumptions and landed thinking he had found a flock of himself. It's also said he needed glasses. In either case the result was the same.

Theodore Skimmer immediately divulged what he'd seen not far away. While skimming the creek in high tide he watched as a human threw food in the air, on the ground and directly at ducks, egret, ibis, blue jay, doves and any flighted creature that paused to watch the scene play out.

The gull laughed at Theodore. They knew better. Humans offer something or toss a thing and then they chase you. It's a trap. Skimmers, they needed to slow down to get the full picture.

"Skimmer you can't believe what you think you saw so easily. How fast did you skim by anyway? She probably chased every one off after you flew back up into the sky. You didn't even see the trap close!"

Theodore realized his species identifying mistake but carried on. His intellect was being challenged. He certainly wasn't leaving until he straightened out a bunch of laughing gulls. They had no self control and very little common sense. "I didn't skim by. I skimmed over, and stopped to watch this phenomenon. You don't see this every day. I tell you she was carefully throwing food in all directions and yelling 'Bello!' while doing it."

"Bello?"

"Yes, Bello. I have no idea what that means. Human language is tedious on it's simplest day."

The gulls laughed, one by one adding to the cacophony in the shade of a parking lot. Some shifted position to laugh harder and get their heads into the headwinds properly. Laughing gulls and their flocks are not made up of a pecking order. They are the Borg in nature. A collective instinct that looks to each member equally as to when to laugh harder. No one wants to be the first to laugh, you could come off looking rather stupid. The laughing subsided. No one wants to be the first to stop laughing either. You could come off looking completely clueless. Banner stepped into the conversation. A laughing gull prone to serious thought and known to be the last bird laughing.

"Alright then Skimmer."

"Theodore, but you can call me Ted."

"Alright Ted. Let's say we believe this story and that there is a human throwing food to all without then trying to chase some. Why would a human do that? Hmmm?" Banner leaned into Ted's personal space as an exclamation point, or possibly a comma.

"You want me to explain a human? I avoid them myself. There's no explaining them. I just know what I saw and I saw a human feeding every creature around food and not attempting any sort of capture whatsoever. She was also shouting 'Bello'. I don't think this was a hunting call, or a warning. She seemed pleased with herself, all in all."

A voice called down from above. An osprey on a nest atop a tall light post looked over the edge.

"I can attest to seeing this human. She's out there when the sun rises full, and when the sun is at his highest. Every. Day. I hunt the creek. I have never seen her chase anything away. She's rather odd for a human." The osprey disappeared from sight returning to her nest. It was empty during this season, but she kept busy rebuilding and refining it's quality for the coming spring.

"Well then gull …"

"Benji."

"Well then Benji. You see. I tell the truth."

"You want us to believe that osprey!? She'd eat one of us just as soon as tell us a story!"

The voice above reached down again. "I heard that you gelastic gull!"

Banner shrank having been heard. The gull flock broke out in laughter again this time Franklin was the first to set them off. He was no fan of Banner. Ted rolled his eyes. This whole scenario had taken up far too much time.

"Do as you like you hysterical bunch. I have skimming to accomplish. I told you what I saw. Take it or leave it for the ducks to enjoy." As the laughter died away with Terry being the last to laugh Ted vaulted into the noon day's sun heading to cross bayou canals. There were no laughing gulls there.

That was the day that the laughing gulls of the shopping center fell upon Lisa and her backyard like a horde of trick or treaters on Halloween. Their first visit she counted 41, she thought. They hovered maniacally and were difficult to get a head count on. After the first visit she didn't bother counting.

Jill hopped down to Jack's perch. A lot had changed in his absence. She'd have to explain while pointing a few things out. The gull flew down and into the backyard harassing Lisa as they do. She didn't skip a beat or a Bello. It was closer to 2 o'clock than noon. The odds of her marauding trick or treating gulls was high.

"About a week after you left Todd and I started coming here. We missed you, and just felt compelled. We didn't bother your human though. But we did come back to keep an eye on her and make sure no crow made any mistaken ideas about claiming your tree. That's when she started feeding a duck. A duck began visiting. Cornelia was her name I think. Every day she would sit on the deck and feed Cornelia. Then Cornelia met a guy in the next neighborhood and she stopped visiting. But obviously she told some other ducks because a few days later there were eleven ducks waiting for her! And she fed them, too. But you know, she always looked up in this tree before she fed anyone. She looked for you, first."

"She looked for me?" Jack blushed a bit. Had she actually looked for him?

"She always looks for you first. So as the ducks starting adding up, she had close to 38 of them visiting, so did all the others. Stiltz and Legs starting visiting. Legs brought the rest of their flock. Then the blue jays started visiting. A few crows I never did meet, they seemed to be passing through. A great egret called Horace. Nice guy. Judgmental, but agreeable. It's what you see now. The gulls show up just often enough to get a good feed, but not often enough to become a problem. I'm amazed at how gull know how disagreeable they can be in large groups. So self aware."

Jack looked out on the scene. He could see Butters through the window. She seemed to be watching the same scene in her backyard. He wondered what she was thinking about all the commotion. Three ducks hopped onto the deck and out of view, hidden by the tin roof.

"The ducks go on the deck!?"

Jill laughed a bit at his panic. "Oh yes, there are times so many ducks are on that deck there isn't room for one more. They take naps mostly. And wait. Are you hungry? I'm hungry. You could introduce me to her. I've never said hello. I didn't think it appropriate without you."

The gulls patience waned at no human throwing food. They began leaving the backyard and backyard air space in small groups. Each laughing out in frustration at the meal that did not materialize. The last two gulls flew over Jack and Jill's position, calling insults toward the house. The air was quiet again. A breeze replaced the litany of gulls.

"I am hungry. Let's see if she's home."

Jack dropped out of the tree extending his wings to guide a smooth landing on the table in front of the window where Butters looked out. Jill arrived just after and just to Jack's left. She looked over her shoulder to see all the wildlife grazing and waiting. No one seemed in any rush. They all drifted quietly between each other, lingering. Their wanderings did not match their voices though. The ducks hissed and honked letting the others know they they hadn't eaten yet either. The blue jays spent their waiting time bullying the starlings. Calling out sounds of human bells and whistles. The doves meticulously searched the ground for morsels left from the last time. Horace Egret kept his distance on the other side of the fence. No point in being bumped and jostled by a bunch of ducks.

Jill looked through the windows. She'd never been this close to a human's house before. It was bright in this room. There were birds in this room. She sucked in her breath surprised to see such colorful beings happily climbing on and over human objects. One chewed on things Jill was certain didn't belong to him at all.

"What are those?"

Jack grinned remembering his own bewilderment when he met Crackers for the first time. Butters looked straight at Jack and screamed. "YOU!"

"Hi in there Butters!"

"YOU! You have been not here for a long time. Did you know my mom keeps looking for you? Why didn't you look back? Who's that with you?"

Jill stepped back behind Jack. This bird talked too fast and this bird saw her. None of that made any sense, yet.

"I was gone. I'm back." Jack remembered she liked to keep things simple and did his best to oblige Butters. "This is Jill. She's a friend."

"Oh. Okay."

Butters flew out of the room without another word.

"That was just plain rude."

"Jill that's a macaw, I met one before her a long time ago. Macaws don't seem to care what others think. They seem to care about what they think of others though. She's alright. Her name is Butters and she is a favorite of my human. So there's a thing to respect here."

Jill walked back around to join Jack looking in the windows. There was a another macaw bird in there. A red one. And one on the far side. Grey. And a little blue one who flew back and forth and back and forth. Screaming something about bananas.

"You inherited a very interesting human, Jack." She looked around the table top. Walking to inspect objects, hopping on the tops of the chairs. She jumped into the pot full of shells. "Hey! These are the shells you use to order food, right?" She picked through them inspecting their size, shape and weight.

"I used to, yes. But it got to the point where she was bringing out things whether I payed or not. I just stopped paying altogether."

"What? She didn't care? You didn't care about your rudeness?

It's only right pay, Jack. You aren't a barbarian." She kicked a smaller shell to the side to reveal a pill bug hidden underneath. She ate him.

Behind them in the yard the waiting crowd began to get restless. One of the ducks had caught a glimpse of Lisa walking in and out of the room. She'd seen them all. The time was growing near.

Lisa began counting heads when she caught sight of Jack on the back deck. Jack was back! She could barely contain herself. And he brought a new friend. Not Barbosa, not Twigg, not Edgar. This was a girl, judging by the size of her. Maybe that was the reason for his absence, girlfriends can be distracting.

Lisa immediately turned back into the hallway to make a quick crow snack before handling the others. She wanted to say hi to Jack, and to his girl. She didn't have a minute to waste. The opportunity could be far shorter than she knew. Lisa made four flax crackers of peanut butter smear with sliced grapes. She grabbed four almonds and a bit of chopped apple from Kirby's plate. No time to loose, she could make more for Kirby later. She quick stepped back into the bird room and gently opened the door onto the deck. She did not want to scare Jack or his girl.

"Hi Jack! I am so happy to see you again! And you brought a friend, too. I'll call you Jill, if you don't mind. I have lunch for you."

"Jack how does she know my name?"

"I don't know. She knows my father and mother's names as well. She knew mine. Sometimes I think she reads minds. You should say hello back though. She enjoys that."

Not wanting to offend a human so important to her friend, Jill called out a crows kindest regards. Jill hopped a bit closer to Jack as well. Making clear she was with him and glad to be there.

"It's nice to meet you too, Jill. Well I've got your favorite Jack. Peanut butter on flax crackers with grapes and almonds. I have to feed the ducks and ibis, too. So I won't spend too much time bothering you. But I am so very glad you are back. I hope you stay awhile. The backyard just isn't the same without your voice."

Lisa laid out the snacks evenly and widely over the table top to give Jack and Jill room to hop around while eating. She went back into the house to make a duck and ibis lunch. Which was left over parrot foods, chopped vegetables and fruits she'd given to the parrots as well. Rice. Popcorn. Blue berries. Sliced grapes. It varied from day to day depending on what the parrots left behind. Lisa was content knowing nothing went to waste at their home. What wasn't eaten by ducks and ibis was eaten by starlings, song birds, passing through crows and squirrels. At night a possum would finish whatever still lay out. Once in a while, Lisa would find a raccoon carrying off the last orange slice. She took note and created a hidden spot for the possum and raccoon to forage in the middle of the night.

Lisa went through the door leading to the deck where Jack and Jill were still eating. She smiled and walked past them to step down onto the grass. There all her neighborhood Muscovy surrounded her waiting for her to spread the left overs. The ibis flew down from the fence top and wondered reluctantly and impatiently for her to begin the feeding.

Jill stopped eating to watch all her neighbor creatures happily interact with Jack's human. She saw her throw the contents of a yellow bowl by fistfuls in all directions. She paid close attention to those that didn't get a fair portion and moved through the crowd of ducks calling each one by a given name. Every bird eating had a name. Every bird there was important to this human. She watched Jack's human wonder carefully between ibis and ducks to spread a full bowl of foods to all. She came back to the deck, and sat on the edge. And there she offered sliced grapes from the bottom of the bowl, and chopped water melon rinds from a second bowl she held underneath the yellow one. A dozen ducks came to her and took their portion from her hand without pause. Jill looked to Jack and back to the hand feeding. It's not ever day you see a Muscovy duck walk up to a human and take food from their hands.

"Jack. I don't know what to say. She's not quite a human, but not quite one of us."

"Do you like your lunch?"

"Oh yes! It's delicious. It's all perfect. I sure do like this peanut butter."

Jack and Jill finished all their portions but one cracker. A squirrel popped up from under the table.

"Hi. Yeah can I have that?"

"Jill are you full?"

"Oh yes, I am stuffed!"

"Well squirrel, it's all yours."

"Oh! Yayaya. Great."

With one twitch and a snatch the squirrel disappeared with the cracker under the table. He reappeared at the edge of the deck and then bolted to the tree at the corner of the yard, and disappeared into the foliage above.

Jack laughed. If that squirrel had stayed put, his human would have brought more food out just for him. Squirrels were just too twitchy for their own good.

Lisa ran out of grapes and water melon. She also ran out of hungry ducks. They were all near or heading to the water bowls she left out for them. They would preen a bit, drink a bit and then congregate under the boat. The trailer put the boat at just the right height for muscovy to walk under and rest from the heat of the day. She and her husband joked about their world's most expensive duck deck. They felt guilty for taking it out some days. The ducks wouldn't have a deck to nap under while they were gone.

She stood up and turned around to find Jack and Jill each perched on a separate chair back. Their crops full. Their eyes a bit sleepy. It was then she noticed her ibis flock burst from the back lot behind her yard. They had finished first and continued to forage in the empty lot behind her fence. Something had spooked them. Ibis spook early for safety.

What bothered them was a group of kids, five in all. Four boys and one girl. They were making their way from the sidewalk a few hundred feet away, heading to the creek. The girl had a net. The youngest boy had a bucket. The other boys had nothing in their hands, and from their attitudes and voices, not much more in their heads.

Lisa bristled. These kids came once week to wreak havoc in the creek catching fry and other small creatures. She had a conversation with them through her fence. The young girl had an aquarium at home. Her parents wouldn't get her proper fish, so she took them from the creek. When they died, she would come back for more.

She had done her best to tell the kids how they were affecting the local land, wild life and food chain. She'd taken an hour of her time to answer questions kindly and honestly. After that last visit she hadn't felt confident. The boys were dismissive and the girl was adamant about wanting fish, and a turtle if she could catch it. She didn't care much at all about any thing construed as a ramification. In her opinion, she wanted it, and she'd take it.

Seeing them back caused Lisa's blood pressure to go up, and her heart to ache. They were marauders and thieves. It hurt to watch them, and she had no choice but to watch and try to to communicate.

"Jack she seems upset about them."

"Yes, she does. Let's get into the tree. For safety sake. She seems pretty tense."

Lisa watched as Jack and Jill lit onto the top of the pine tree. She looked at the five children entering the creek haphazardly. Dread built up in her throat. Eleven and twelve years of age and clueless, even after being told. Her ducks were safe from their arrogant disregard. Her crow watched from above. She had to try one more time.

"Hi guys, back for more fish?"

The boys didn't bother to look at her. They were busy scrambling at the edge of the creek trying to push each other into the water. The tide was low. Any one falling in would find themselves embedded in a good foot of briny mud and muck. The young girl looked over.

"Yeah. I want to get some of those striped fish I saw. My other ones died too fast."

"Ah! So basically you just keep killing fish and keep coming back for more. You're killing fish that could feed a dolphin one day. You're killing fish that can and do feed the small turtles, shore birds that visit here and other fish. You are killing fish other creatures need to live. Climbing all over the edge of the creek destabilizes the vegetation and harms the small environment hundreds of insects live in. And those are the insects the frogs and turtles need to live. You're all just killing things."

Lisa's head pounded slightly. She hated waste. She hated selfish human behavior and she thoroughly hated repeating herself. She'd said all this the last time. Only kinder without all the barbs.

The youngest boy defending himself against the other three's pushes and shoves scrambled up to the top of the edge. "I'm killing bugs and things?" Truth hurts and heals at the same time.

"Yes, yes you are, all of you."

The other followed suit and climbed out of the creek. One of the boys shoes were covered in mud, his ankles caked as well.

One of them also had rocks in both hands. Taken from the bottom of the creek. They were slick, and covered in blackness. They dripped muck and water from his hands. Four boys stood looking at Lisa through her fence. Only one seemed to actually hear and care.

The girl continued fishing with her net. Depositing fish in the bucket the youngest boy had set near her. She looked and counted her catch. She looked up and over to Lisa. She looked at Lisa with a stare that made it clear she did not care what an adult had to say or think about what she was doing. She reached down again with her net trying to scoop more fish. "Get over here and help me!"

The youngest boy walked over to hold the half filled bucket containing the next batch of fry destined to die within a day. For no good reason at all. Lisa bristled. The girl showed no emotion accept intent.

The three remaining boys grew bored. Bored with adults watching. Bored with their younger friends doing something that drew the attention of the adult watching. They began shoving each other and hurling insults as they did. Lisa looked up to see Jack and Jill had made their way down the tree a few branches.

"Jack we should go."

"Why? We're safe up here."

"Yes, I know, but this is all looking, human."

"One thing I've learned about humans, they all look uncomfortably human most of the time. I'm not so sure they know how happy they could be if they'd just stop half of what they're doing."

Lisa looked at the three boys with no direction or purpose and the boy and girl with misplaced purposes. Her brain was telling her to go in the house and leave it all alone. She looked over her shoulder to the ducks. Settled, nestled and watching. If they cared she couldn't tell. She looked up to her crow. What do creatures such as they think when seeing all this stupidity. They must have witnessed it before in another place. Do humans look as lost as she felt at that very moment?

She looked back at the kids she lived near but didn't know very well. They didn't seem to have concerns or cares she'd had at their age. That very thought made her laugh out loud. She sounded like her parents. How embarrassing.

"What's your name?" Lisa looked at the tallest boy holding the rocks. She'd not met him.

He looked at her with suspicion. Fair enough since he didn't have a clue who she was or why should would care to know. "I'm Lisa." She offered her name first, in hopes of leading with a smile.

"Joe." He said it with purpose and a laugh. They all laughed. His name wasn't Joe.

"Okay Joe. What do you know?" She'd hoped to somehow laugh with them a bit and whittle a moment of humanity. Humanity is not an easy thing to whittle out of humans.

The youngest boy holding the bucket yelled out, "That's not his name!"

"SHUT UP!"

Jill flew to the top of the pine. She wanted to be as far away from that voice as possible. Jack stayed where he was, watching. He couldn't help himself. He'd enjoyed watching all the humans on the other side. He always learned something new by watching. Ardon had once said watching a human and remembering what they did or did not was the safest way to learn what not to do around them.

Gregory mentioned watching humans just wasted time better spent watching grass grow. There was nothing to learn at all. Which is why he kept his behind facing them most of the time.

Jack watched his human. He couldn't agree with Gregory. He watched his human try to teach young humans. Tanner would be surprised. He watched his human's shoulders fall just a little. Was she feeling defeated? Misunderstood? Hated? Ignored? Or was she needing a nap. It was all hard to say. He couldn't look away. There was something to know here.

The boy with the rocks looked at Lisa. "Why do you want to know my name?"

"It makes it a lot easier to have a conversation, and if I see you again I can say hello properly."

The boys laughed and shook their heads. "Whatever. I don't even know you. And maybe I don't want to."

"Fair enough. I'm just trying to be nice. That doesn't mean you have to try to be nice." Lisa's shoulders lowered a little bit more. Where do you go in a conversation when the other person already has eyes so cold and hard.

He turned around and spoke quietly to the other two boys. What he said had them all laughing even harder. Lisa noticed the girl had gotten out of the creek rather quickly and was gathering her bucket, jar, and net. She grabbed the younger boy by the shoulder and spun him around. "Let's go. Now."

She didn't look at Lisa, but the boy did. "I'm sorry. I didn't know this was hurting the animals. I won't do this again cause now I know." Lisa smiled to him. One out of five isn't bad in the grand scheme of things.

Jack watched the boy and his human and how they smiled to each other. He remembered a boy and his mother back on the other side. The boy had thrown his drink cup on the ground and was walking away from it when his mother stopped him. She pointed to the cup and asked him why he would do such a thoughtless thing. She had asked him how many cups would be laying around if every one there did the same thing? Jack remembered the boys face twist from solving the question to shock, when the answer came. He had lowered his head and answered his mother. Too many. He then walked to his cup, picked it up and put it where it belonged in a can. She smiled at him and thanked him. He smiled to her without a word.

Some humans were smarter than others. Some humans learned the first time. And it seemed when one learned from another they both were happier for it. There was something to know from this, he leaned out from his branch continuing to watch the humans below. Jill wasn't as impressed or as certain. "Jack, come up here and watch."

"In a second. I can't see their faces from up there. There's a lot to see in a human face." Gregory would have disagreed. Tanner would say it made no difference one way or the other.

Lisa walked down the fence to stand parallel to the boy with the slick black rocks in his hands. She had a passing question in her head. Why hang onto them? But her goal to win a bit of confidence in the boy ran right over that thought. If she could get them to understand the impact of their actions she felt confident they would think twice about it the next opportunity. She looked up at Jack Crow perched three quarters up the pine tree. Jill was at the top crowing to him. Animals were easier. Creatures of nature were a balanced element rather than a clambering human running into things without regard. Humans had no interest in balance. Just control.

The boy with the handful of rocks followed her gaze to the crow. This woman and all her talk about animals and nature and whatever needing whatever. None of what he was doing was any of her business. This wasn't her yard. He hated adults sticking their nose into things that don't belong to them.

Maybe he just hated adults. He looked at his two friends who were busy watching this woman. They looked like they were waiting on her to talk more. He wanted her to say nothing at all.

Casandra and her brother were halfway to the sidewalk with her bucket of stupid fish. That woman was right, those fish were gonna die in her stupid tank on the stupid table in her bedroom. He almost felt like telling this woman that they were gonna die for sure. She was right about that part.

Then he saw something more interesting. That crow was looking at that woman. He was really looking at her.

Stupid crow. Without a thought and without much effort the boy took a quick aim and fell back with his handful of rocks to throw them as hard as he could at that crow. Right now, he hated that crow and he wanted it to die like the fish. He didn't care. Why should he? He released the handful of slick cold rocks into the air directed right at that crow. He caught his forward motion with a step forward and he waited to see if he'd get the bird, before the bird knew what he'd done. Stupid crow.

Jack watched Lisa scream and reach out toward the boy. He heard her shout, "No!" before he knew anything else. Before he'd heard her he saw her face. He saw hope, then fear. Her face changed so quickly he wasn't quite sure he'd seen anything change at all.

"NO!" Lisa's shock ran down the length of her body and entered the earth below. She stood leaning on her toes reaching for the rocks that flew threw the air missile straight. "WHY? No!" She ran. Her mind screamed in on itself. Her eyes didn't leave the projectiles heading toward Jack. Her Jack watched her. He turned his head slightly intrigued. She'd never come out of the gate before.

The three boys laughed and pointed and waited to see the end results. Lisa waited for nothing but an answer to why. Jack heard the no, and felt a thud against his wing. Another against his keel bone. A third flew past his head missing him by a feather. The fourth made contact above his left eye. He heard his human scream, "WHY!?" He'd never heard her voice like that before. Jack looked up to see Jill crowing and taking wing to fly in a circle toward him. He felt air rushing up against his body. He. Was falling.

Lisa ran to position herself under Jack. Time crawled. How time slowed she did not care, she did care that somehow she could catch her friend before he would hit the ground. She turned her attention in those seconds to life rather than hate. She heard the boys laughing. She heard herself cry.

Jack's wings wouldn't work. His sight didn't work. He only heard the winds rushing up against him, the voice of Jill calling, and the voice of his human friend begging to know why. He felt it all, he heard it all. And it all began fading to black.

Lisa fell to the ground on her knees under Jack's descending body. She could catch him, she just needed to focus. Jack could hear her crying. He heard Jill calling. He heard the winds fighting over his direction and felt none of them win.

Lisa grabbed the end of her shirt and made a hammock to catch Jack's falling body. The weight of his arrival and the span of his open wing was shocking. Far away he seemed so fragile. Now with him cradled in her arms and shirt he felt strong but injured. His eyes were closed. His right wing loose and broken. His left wing opened fully, revealing no damage. His head showed blood at the point of impact. Lisa looked upon ruined staggering beauty. She felt rage and hate.

Jack could only hear Jill's calls, and over those, his human demanding to know why. Why would he do this to her crow. Why? He didn't move within her embrace. He didn't because he couldn't. Somewhere along his body he lost the ability to ask anything of his physical self. He laid in her arms feeling her warmth and her anger.

"WHY? Why would you do such a thing? How could you think to do even do such a thing? Are you that evil? Is that who you are? A murderer, like your friend over there?" Lisa's rage translated into words unabridged. Her filter gave way to her utter hopeless sadness. It's all so fragile. Too fragile. Not enough care about the fragile nature of simple perfections. The boys had stopped laughing. Casandra and her brother stood on the sidewalk watching. Shame? Shock? Lisa couldn't read their faces that far away. She could barely breath for it all.

The boy who threw the rocks. The boy who stood still now dropping the remaining rocks from his left hand, said nothing. The two others had run off before Jack had fallen into Lisa's shirt. They were on the sidewalk as well. Lisa looked into the eyes of the boy who murdered a crow for no reason. His eyes were open wide, and empty. They lacked understanding. They lacked a why. Two brown eyes unable to focus on the details of what they had accomplished. He stood still. She kneeled holding a treasure he had no right to look upon. Lisa quietly cried, exhausted by the lack of empathy around her.

Jack hadn't heard the answer to her question of why. He lay unable to move, and aware of everything. More aware than he'd been able to muster before. The boy had no why at all. He felt sorry for him. Jack had found so many different versions of why over these last seasons. Why was easy. Finding a why turned out to be the easy half of life. Once you chose your why the hard part began. You had to live up to your why. You had to live up to it and share it with every one you loved. And you had to accept that some of those you cared about may find your why to be, senseless. A why they couldn't accept themselves. He felt bad for his human. She needed the boy's why to make sense out of this moment. But there was no why because the boy had never chosen one.

Why. At this moment Jack realized why didn't matter, and he didn't want one. You needed a why to travel life.

You didn't need a why to leave.

Made in the USA
Lexington, KY
20 November 2019

57354736R00141